MICHAEL'S IVY

KEITH BINGHAM

INDIES UNITED PUBLISHING HOUSE, LLC

Published July 2020
by Indies United Publishing House, LLC

Second Edition

Cover art by irPanda

ISBN: 978-1-64456-154-6
Library of Congress Control Number: 2020939784

INDIES UNITED PUBLISHING HOUSE, LLC
P.O. BOX 3071
QUINCY, IL 62305-3071
www.indiesunited.net

Dedicated to Jeff Burnsides

CHAPTER 1

There are four main points of which I am sure of in the progression of my life:

I am a criminal.
I will stand trial for crimes against humanity.
I have no defense, I will simply state the crime humanity appears to be.
All things are subjective.

I am accused of being a terrible inter-dimensional drug dealer, of destroying the fabric of society and tearing apart the veil of life that governs existence, of passing around a poisonous plant like so much candy and condemning otherwise innocent lives.

You would think, having done what I've done, I would understand the length and breadth of my actions.

Since there are questions on Earth I won't answer, I will be shipped back to Horizon, which is the dimension this drug comes from. I have been asked repeated questions. Where in Horizon did I find Bloodleaf? Who helped me bring it to Earth? Why in God's name did I do it?

Earth has yet to adopt laws governing what I've done, so I will be sent to Horizon for trial, which, again, is an infinite new dimension and a brand new world. I am to serve as an example, it seems. Humanity is earnest to have me answer for my crimes as long as I am alive.

The plant Bloodleaf is instantly and terminally addictive upon ingestion. There is no experimenting with Bloodleaf. You can't take the drug for recreation. When you dose, your body will grow into a perfect and pristine state of health. Old scars will fade, any wounds you have will heal and you will be physically healthier than you have ever been and ever really could be otherwise.

However, a few days later, your blood will boil inside your skin if you do not take it again. Your flesh will start to fall away from the bone over the course of an hour or so. You will die painfully, in agony, as long as you are still breathing.

I've seen, and so know, this is a terrible way to die. Since I will be needed alive for a trial and my conviction, Global Security and Safety is allowing me to continue to take a plant they have officially classified as a poison.

Life, itself, is a terrible poison and none of it ever mattered. I made no choices about what I was born into. I make no claims that existence is not the product of some horribly massive heat death or some other powerful energy to which life desperately clings.

There are no Gods, there is no secret goodness guiding us through life, there is no gated community at the end of a bright blue tunnel. Mankind continuously searches for meaning, blind to the reality of their own mind as they speak it, dying in search of their own vision as they make it.

We were launched into a playground of physics and given nightmares for brains, constantly seeking support in an otherwise meaningless existence, one where our best societies are determined by the suppression of others. We inflict upon each other our own internal psychoses, our own thoughts and feelings, which have no value other than how much they are supported by others. Even in this, we only paint a picture of a world as we would like to see it or believe it is. It is an illusionary function, yet still, millions die without any support for their views, or the ability to support others. They die in the name of disease, starvation, or war and we call it 'evolution' or 'Darwin's Law', or whatever convenient name we can come up with.

One of the tricks I face from Bloodleaf is it's hard to ever really die from anything. You heal every time you eat it, so I will live as long as I take Bloodleaf and only die if I stop.

I will be forced to take it once I'm imprisoned. It can literally be shoved down my throat for as long as I have one and I will live. When I am sentenced to life imprisonment, you had better believe it will be served. It simply isn't enough that I've committed a terrible crime, I will be punished and made to answer to the human race.

Horizon is a dimension that has only recently been discovered in the dark and murky history of mankind and Bloodleaf is native to it. A group of Earth scientists, through the proof of the atomic nature of existence and the subsequent research surrounding it, hypothesized that our own reality was woven and nestled into the fabric of another dimension.

They published their research detailing their work and pointed to tantalizing clues left within other leading scientific publications in support of this new and radical idea.

Before you could say, *Black Helicopters,* the entire research group and the actual scientists themselves simply might as well have not existed.

If anyone had looked into what had transpired, they would have found certain companies quietly purchased, dissolved and shifted in other directions through various funding channels.

Simply put, several governments on the planet knew of this new dimension's existence. Specifically, several groups of key individuals within these varying governments were already aware of the dimension's existence and working on the issues involved.

During the next few decades, the research organized around the existence of this new dimension was kept hidden from the general population, even among the collaborative efforts between the respective groups and governments as well.

That might be as long as the human race can keep a secret from itself, a few decades. Other groups and individuals started to theorize, understand, and eventually prove the existence of this inner or outer world, and before long, the cat was simply out of the bag for everyone. Hallelujah.

It was Switzerland who made the first official public declaration of the existence of a new dimension and the stance they adopted in regards to it was, unsurprisingly, neutrality.

Of course, this political position towards a brand new frontier became a hallmark of the human race and it subtly, quietly, and universally changed the ethos and principles of the dominant nations on Earth. It fundamentally altered the collective unconscious of all living generations from that point forward, for one simple reason: The people of Earth had finally discovered what they suspected all along, of all the planets, the solar system, the Milky Way, and all the universe as we could perceive, conceive, and prove, we were only a very small part of a much larger place.

Through a worldwide and political stance of neutrality, we were shown the nature of being confronted with the thought of freedom and a new land. We were hypnotized, cold, and calculating.

There was another realm behind or inside the mathematical curtain of our existence. The physics of our universe were ultimately shown to be a series of Russian doll sets nestled within themselves. They were nothing more than the eternal layers of an onion, any which way you sliced it. In spite of our fears, it proved there was no deviation in our fated lives. All of time existed in its entirety in our universe.

Life in our dimension grew its way in and out and all around this unchanging fabric. It suffered and wept for change from its unchangeable nature. Our math reflected it, our art reflected it, and our very lives reflected this. We were imprisoned, sensed it, and couldn't tell how.

What could be beyond this curtain of an infinitely repetitive reflection, an eternally unchanging world of energy, and plants, and rocks, even life? The truth of existence. Earth and our universe were only a captured image of an outer plane. We were a reflection of something much greater, but worse, we were some kind of fragment of a larger piece, only a breath of life on it.

The ground did not wrap back around itself in this new

dimension, like it does on Earth. It teemed with flora and fauna and other mysteries that had never been conceived. This dimension, where we would eventually set foot, would be called Horizon.

I have never understood why most of the people I've spoken with about Horizon were fearful, apprehensive, superstitious, or even angry under the surface. As I eventually came to find out, it wasn't Horizon they truly felt these emotions for, it was other people. Their thoughts trickled through a hazy filter of power and disbelief and this was how myths were born.

We didn't discover a way out of our imprisonment until recently. Somehow, a gateway was built on Earth, and it was there you could exit out of the dimension we were in. You couldn't fly, you couldn't swim, you couldn't wish it so, but you could take a boat to an island called 'Avalon', in honor of a story from Earth's history, long ago, and if you made it that far, you could use a gateway.

It wasn't that easy, at first. A field emanated from the gateway with the distinction of making your deeply held thoughts and emotions start manifesting in reality before you ever reached the gateway on the Earth side.

This startling phenomenon initially made finding the island, much less getting anywhere near the gateway itself, a challenge. A researcher hired by a military convoy is considered to be the first person to set foot on the island.

He stated a large creature was telling him it was a friend to the original creator of the universe. It also said there was, indeed, such a gateway that allowed one to leave this dimension, but warned it would broadcast an energy field where thoughts and feelings of anyone nearby would manifest themselves into reality. The scientist went on to say the creature held a striking resemblance to a stuffed toy he'd cherished as a child. One he kept with him until the day it became lost during a move into a new home. As a child, he eventually imagined it had gone off to be with God and then the man went on to say he had always wondered what God looked like, and after having said this, the transmission with the crew ended.

Despite early evidence to the contrary, it was later

established that the ocean and land around the gateway would manifest a reality based on the thoughts and feelings of individuals nearby. After some time, the American government discovered a way to get to, and through, the gateway on Avalon.

Certain people, called Dreamers, had a particularly unique set of characteristics which heightened their empathy to almost superhuman levels. They felt so much and to such a great complexity, their thoughts and feelings would envelope those of others around them, and only the Dreamer's internal reality would be reflected when near the gateway.

This allowed groups of people to travel safely to the island without fear of everything dissolving into a chaotic and uncontrolled nightmare of individual neurosis.

Dreamers were highly sought. When found, a Dreamer would be cast into a new "liberated" type of indentured servitude, since their abilities were priceless. The Dreamer, and their families, were removed from the burden of providing for their own care or needs and were honored throughout the entirety of the world.

Their brain structure, nervous system, and other essential biological and physiological traits were carefully analyzed and measured for how many people could safely travel in their presence. They were kept in containment on the decks of ships and given chemicals and drugs so the very cells of their bodies and minds would hum and vibrate in a blissful and calm purgatory, ensuring the world surrounding the gateway would reflect back seas that were quiet, tranquil, and calm. The island would do no harm and passengers would make it safely through the gateway to the other side, without fear.

Over the years, as the number of Dreamers grew, a loose consortium of traveling ships arose, bringing the cost of travel into the realm of the idle rich. Several ships were available for passage, each with its own Dreamer. The elite, the richest, the cream of the crop of all of Earth's societies would eventually be afforded passage, or be invited to travel, on a somewhat regular basis.

They would bring back to Earth tales of wonder, new technologies, thoughts and ideas, and would be rewarded with highly prized social esteem and loyalty.

Maybe that's why I did it.

I was asked how I had learned about the drug, how I brought it to Earth and who else had taken the plant, or had access to one. Since I would not answer questions to incriminate myself, I would be sent to New Civ for trial.

New Civ is the first settlement built in Horizon. It is geared largely as a resort area and center of operations for wealthy travelers to assist with funding and building within Horizon.

Several interest groups have established themselves in New Civ and are somewhat unified in their efforts of studying the surrounding area and developing the city. A hired police force keeps protection and assists with rescue efforts in the area. There is also a small serving class of restaurants, theater, entertainment, and whatever else money and limited seating entices people with, all in a strange and unknown frontier. It is a prim, little city, with a relaxed set of laws.

I was informed I was to be sent on the first available ship traveling to Avalon, so I asked for freedom to move about the ship, asylum during my travel, and a pony.

It didn't matter what I asked for, I had no options. The soldiers tasked with arresting me had aimed their rifles and loudly told me to get down on the ground and put my hands outward because I was an unsolvable monster who had damned the human race.

A weapon was never much out of my sight during the time after I was apprehended. I don't believe anyone would have used one, considering I was to be kept alive for what would be a public trial.

I had challenged and invalidated humanity's souls and salvation because I could never die and I had given the plant to others who would also not die, as long as they had access to the plant.

Political machines jumped into action after my arrest. The American government classified Bloodleaf as an addictive poison. With the help of Global Security and Safety, I was to be tried for crimes against humanity.

I was dragged through the media as a monster. My words were twisted so that I was shown and proved to be dangerous. Whatever my objection, I was dangerous, and through my actions I had brought danger to society itself.

The public merely wished me death, but this was impossible by now, from them or for myself. What manifested towards me, instead, was a deep, black, instinctual fear. I would need to be convicted of a crime and put to death under proof of guilt, according to the law. Any time they wished, I could have Bloodleaf taken from me, but this was paramount to ending my life.

Keep talking, Michael, the officials cooed. Keep eating those leaves, buddy.

The people wished me strung up, they wished to fire arrows into my heart, but most of all they wanted justice, which meant men needed to understand the gravity of the situation and create new laws regarding what I'd done and what I had introduced into society.

Horizon was immensely important to everyone and I was the first to introduce something tangible and unexpected from outside of our dimension.

In a way, again, anyone's idea of compassion, and what it might mean towards me, wanted nothing short of my death, but more importantly, humanity wanted to be free of me, innocent of any guilt they might share, while convicting me of my own personal tragedies.

By sending me to Horizon for trial, a precedent could be set for both worlds. I was to be given a life sentence, remain on Bloodleaf, unable to die, and serve as a reminder to humanity of the consequences of the actions I had taken.

They placed me in a part of the ship with a group of people who were artists, painters, and other aesthetic craftsmen. They had been commissioned to experience the new world and return to share it with others.

Bloodleaf has another side effect which I alluded to earlier.

You can read the minds of others soon after dosing, usually for ten minutes to half an hour. You could even see through another person's eyes for a length of time, should that person take Bloodleaf as well.

This was how I knew what the officials of Global Security and Safety had planned for me, and what led to my refusal to answer questions, my solace in the Fifth Amendment, a right which would be taken from me in a new land.

It was thought that artists, being more "sensitive" to their own mental processes, would make good trustees and were informed to alert anyone if I should begin to exercise my ability to read minds in any capacity to try and free myself either through mental manipulation or coercion. This was a confusing issue, as it was thought I could manipulate minds, and this tactic was used during the political process to promote fear of what I had done.

I reclined in my cot, chewing lightly on Bloodleaf, and let my mind wander and fuzz as it opened to the dim thought-chatter of the cruise ship. I could see a total of 327 people aboard. I've always known this easily, and as far as I know, I've been the only one with this gift to accurately know the number of people in my range. Many were crew members, judging by the shared content of their thoughts. I continued as my psyche spread throughout the ship, opening to their minds. Surprisingly, or not, in the room directly above, two travelers were passionately embracing and making love. They were married to other people. I could see they each thought the other was traveling alone as they spun each other thoughts of other lives and other identities.

Lying back, my awareness spread to its limit and my body tense like a drum, a whisper appeared in my mind.

"Save me," the voice said. The waters of my awareness smoothed and funneled, making room for the words.

"You. You can save me," the voice said.

I had never been reached this way.

"Please. I sensed you just now. The guards believe I am more induced than I am. We're entering the field of the gateway. The effects of my stasis are not as strong and I am more aware than normal. I had thought for... I've influenced the guards into mild dreams... daydreams... but now they are asleep. Please, come up here. You can, safely. All you need is to enter a password nearby, it's the lock to my stasis. I don't want to be here. I can't live the rest of my life like this and I believe it will not be too long before I am put under. You are my only chance, please."

A wave washed over my consciousness and splashed into my soul, heavy with despair and annihilation. A deep misery and sadness with a dull, blind ache of narcotics and I knew it was the Dreamer of our ship. Despite the haze, the thoughts and words that came into my mind were strong and sophisticated in presence. They pierced me, yet they were as slippery and feathery as a short and oiled stiletto knife. Her feelings were of long isolation and absolutely no perception of an end or freedom.

I quietly thought of choices. Here I am, on my way to stand trial for a life sentence and she wanted me to free her from her own.

So, I carefully got up and made my way out through the main door, my consciousness stretching thin and brittle, my limbs and muscles tense and taut. She was a fellow prisoner. Who am I to refuse a plea for freedom? What could I lose?

As far as my mind could reach, I could sense the passengers and crew falling asleep or already sleeping. The passengers were entering their dreams, their minds were soft, my own was eased.

Quickly, I found my way to the deck. The boat was near enough to the island that the field from the gateway was stronger, enveloping the Dreamer's reality more so. I went through the door I needed, seeking and feeling her, stopping at the large containment unit at the end of the room, against the wall.

Placing my hands on the capsule, I peered through the glass. She was beautiful, with tanned skin, dark black hair, her eyes held a vaguely Asian cast, and her face was splashed with freckles. The capsule uttered gentle beeps and in the soft glow she appeared to be wearing a paper gown.

"Please," she thought. Her eyes were heavily lidded, and she was breathing in short, shallow breaths. "The password is 'KOJI'. Press 'Medical Care'."

The guards were still asleep. I found the terminal I needed, the screen showed nothing more than a blank white entry box and a few selections to the right of this. I entered the password on the keyboard and pressed 'Medical Care' on the screen.

After that, there was no time. I believe I watched her for hours, in that moment, although it passed in the span of several breaths. The capsule opened as my vision seemed to come from a tunnel that was yards away. Somewhere in there, she shrieked and writhed while engulfed in flame. She was a phoenix. She shot out of the capsule, through the ceiling, and she was gone. I reeled and realized manifestations of emotion and thought would soon become reality with her escape. She had been our only tether to a safe existence. The Bloodleaf was beginning to fade and my awareness started to slowly retreat to the safety of my own mind.

I believed everyone to still be asleep. I heard one of the guards mutter and sigh as I hurried out through the door. The moon hung large overhead, bright and white, reflecting it's light on the water which sang and danced back to the sky in a cadence only the ocean and moon know.

Walking on the deck, I started to hear screaming from the sleeping quarters of the passengers. I heard glass shattering and watched several winged shapes drag a woman through a broken window and take flight. She struggled as they pulled at her limbs, tearing at her body and dropping her into the ocean. I looked for the door that would lead me back below deck and heard a shout, "Marsha, how could you? My son! My son is dead!" Several more screams and the ocean began to churn as I heard something loud and heavy crash against a wall. I felt the wood and metal beneath my feet ache and groan as voices set the air ablaze.

Oh, God. The Bloodleaf had left me dizzy. I took another step and fell to the floor as people ran by, the terrors of our own minds as real as the darkness of the night.

In hindsight, I guess all of our underlying fears along with the isolation of the Dreamer had manifested itself into one solid reality, with all of us being so close to the gateway and now unprotected. From the floor of the deck, I saw an immense form begin to rise out of the water. I recognized a head and shoulders, and through the darkness, a single eye. An ethereal weave reached from each of us on the ship and flowed back into that eye. The moonlight gleamed off of its face covered in horns and its teeth curved back for rows as it opened its mouth. A snake-like tongue slit out, polished and cleaned each horn, playing across them in a macabre spiderweb dance. Each horn tied to another fear of a passenger, and we knew this because it knew this.

My teeth chattered and I could not turn my head. I could see its shoulders were heavy and looked as long as the ship. Its skin was translucent through the light of the moon, as several of its organs glowed. It had ropes of immense golden chains and large gemstones hanging from its neck. I covered my face and heard weeping as it began to speak. As it raised a wet dripping fist towards the ship, screams and terror-filled shouting rang out into the night. Its hand and arm were laden with yards of wet, black hair. Its voice was both deep and resonant, yet shrill and high-pitched, piercing our minds. The force of its voice blew the boat back and I rolled. Its tongue moved sharply and whipped as it trilled and chirped in a language older than time. It shrieked of evils done and of horrors untold in countless worlds. Evils that never saw the light of day, cursing all that was alive with a splattering of black cruelty, too unbearable to die, wither, be forgotten, and go where these things go.

Dear God.

I cannot remember anything else. I heard one word out of everything it spoke. It was Michael. It was my own name. I went black. It was the last I could remember.

CHAPTER 2

I was on my back, my eyes were filled with dust, and I started to panic. My muscles were decaying. How long ago did I take Bloodleaf? I'm dying. Oh, dear God, I'm dying. Where am I and what is going on? I need to dose, where's my pack? Where the hell am I? I realize I'm on the ocean. I know this. I can feel the waves. Please, God, let me open my eyes. I can't lift my head. I can't see anything. My life is ebbing. A red tunnel appears, repeating over and over and I am dying.

I think I can move my hands. If I ride the slow lap of the waves below my body, if I rock with the current, I may be able to move my hands.

My head is lying against some bed or bench, or platform it seems. My face feels covered in salt and blistered from the sun. My mouth is dry and my tongue is furry. I can feel my tongue turning to furry meat. My body burns and the pain is unbearable and it feels as if knotty worms are burrowing into my flesh.

Oh, please, God, don't let me die like this, unable to open my eyes and see where I am. It's taking all of my strength and I'm moving my fingers. I should have a satchel, but... I don't know.

Don't vomit, Michael, you've got this. Pulling my arm to my waist, I feel the rough fabric of the satchel holding the dried leaves. A weak spurt of blood and strength splashes through my veins. It runs through the cloying sickness of my limbs as my mind seizes on my last chance at life. I don't want to die. Not now. Not like this. My hand slides in the satchel and I feel the plant material, the familiar texture of the leaves. I take another breath and slowly begin to count each inhale and exhale, building strength and trying to keep conscious. *One.* I push my fingers further in the satchel. *Two.* I clasp my fingers around a dry, leathery leaf.

Three.

Four.

Some moistness returns to my eyes, lips and the tip of my tongue; my body's response to the prospect of being alive. I slit my eyelids and see nothing but red, blinding light.

Five.

I slowly pull a leaf out, ever slowly, ever carefully as I feel my hands bruising and decaying.

Please don't let me die.

My mouth waters and I feel pieces of skin sloughing off the roof of my mouth and behind my nose into my throat.

Six.

Please. Panting, I drag a leaf out of the satchel.

Seven.

My world spirals, thoughts of my life flit by and by, shadows, echoes and impressions of some far-off memories tied together and I move my hand toward my mouth, through nausea, the air turns to jelly and the wind tears at the leaf in my fingertips.

Eight? Nine? I've lost count.

I open my mouth and I feel the crusted blood break on my lips and a warm sticky feeling covers my tongue. Slowly, I chew the head of the leaf. God, I never meant for any of this to happen.

The taste. The taste is bitter and wonderful and horrible and my whole life all at the same time. My skin prickles and my face feels like spun sugar, broken and crystalline, and then like sand caving in and, oh dear, oh dear. I chew carefully and earnestly. In the end, I guess I'm already dead, but I'll live another day.

My teeth chatter as my face flushes. I lick my lips and put the rest of the leaf back in the satchel. I feel my muscles kick, twitch and knit themselves together. After a few moments, my mind starts to open itself dimly as I take erratic breaths of air. I see images. The minds around me are so different from the way I am used to them, yet still familiar. Three people, two male and one female. One of the men has just woken, the other two are asleep or unconscious.

I open my eyes. We are on the ocean in a life raft. The sun beams high, the sky is pale, the water moves with little peaks flowing and rocking infinitely. I look down at myself. My clothes are dry. My skin looks sunburned, but this seems to be fading as the Bloodleaf works its way through the rest of my body. How long have I been adrift on the ocean?

"Three days," comes a voice from the man who has woken. I look over and see him slumped with his head resting uncomfortably and he pulls himself up to his elbows. His hair is dirty blonde, curly, and waves wildly from his head. His lips are chapped and his face is bright red and peeling. He has a rustic look to him. In fact, he looks shipwrecked. The cloth of his white shirt looks salt-washed.

"Just answering your question, friend. Maybe you didn't realize you were talking out loud. You're the prisoner, right? The one from the news? We've been on this raft for three days. I helped get you on it. Here, have some water, you haven't had any."

He tosses a plastic canteen my way and I catch it, still disturbed by the sequence of events. Somewhere in the ghostly and weak flickers of his mind, I see his name is Steven. It's not often I can learn someone's name from their thoughts, and I grasp the opportunity.

"Where is everyone, Steven?"

His eyes widen and he flinches, "So, you do know my name, then. It is true, you read minds." This frightens him. "They're dead or drowned, which means they're dead anyway. We're the only survivors, as far as I know. Why don't you just read my mind and find out what happened?"

He's bewildered but trying to gain ground. It's a common trick people use when they're off guard, get as much information as you can to gain an upper hand either then, or later.

Knowledge is power. I know this because I see his thoughts.

"I can't read memories. I can just see thoughts and ideas," Trying to ease his fear, I say, "Here's your water back and yes, I agree it was a smart move for... Masum to ask you to watch the canteen, thank you."

I recognized the other man on the raft as Masum, one of the artists I'd befriended on the ship. I understood through Steven's thoughts it was Masum who made Steven responsible in some way for getting me onto the life raft, as well as holding the canteen of water. I already knew Masum's name, but I say it like I had learned it from Steven's mind to confuse and intimidate him, if only to stop the questions. He quiets down. I have no desire to eat more Bloodleaf and expect the thought reading to fade soon. I am no longer weary, but this gentleman is and the situation scares him which is making him weaker.

"You were talking to yourself. I was just answering. You've been unconscious." He looks off to the side and snickers. "We were going to throw you overboard, but we knew you were still alive."

"Thanks."

He looks at me. "We were joking about keeping you around to eat you if you died, and if we should wait for you to die, but you were looking pretty shitty." He cracks a large smile at this and his lips split painfully. "You look better than ever now. You really are that prisoner, aren't you? You're the guy with the drug?"

"Yeah." Sometimes I forget that other people can't read my mind. Sometimes I forget that I need to explain things when I'm taking Bloodleaf, but I don't feel like I can do this right now.

"I guess the news was right, you can't die."

I say nothing. I sit back and run my palms along the canvas of the raft. His mind is muted as he focuses on the news he had read and watched.

"What's your name? Or do you just go by 'prisoner'?" he asks.

"It's Michael."

"Michael," he repeats. Satisfied with my answers for now, he lies back and pulls his shirt up over his face, "You should sleep, Michael. Save your strength. We'll be out here awhile, I think."

"Try not to think that," I say, because I realize at this point we are probably still near the gateway, but nothing seemed to be manifesting. I sit back calmly, and as the Bloodleaf begins to wear down, I am aware that both Steven and I have only small ideas and emotions, although they are tangible and hopeful. I realize that it must be Koji, somehow the phoenix is influencing us, even now. Bloodleaf will always make one introspective, as your own deepest thoughts are revealed to your awareness, as well. I know I will never see this woman again. I realize she is the only woman I would have ever wanted to love in my bleak and shattered life and I am surprised. I didn't know her, but her words were desperate, kind and honest. Her feelings now are still desperate, kind and honest, and this is what we are out here.

I then understand that Steven's wife is dying. She swallowed seawater and nearly drowned, and now she bakes in the sun, and because she is dying, Steven wants to ask me to give her Bloodleaf. He wants me to save her with the plant, having witnessed my own regrowth. The problem is that I won't because she doesn't want to live. She wants to die, it is in her psyche, it is in her innermost secrets. She doesn't want to go to Horizon, which is where we are headed. She is living out her last moments in a daze, locked inside her dehydrated and burned body, trying to rectify her past to understand that wherever she is going to go after this, she will be alright because her time in this world or the next is done. I will never subject her to the cruelty of being alive in the same sea of humanity I am doomed to be a part, in whatever role or form, forever, as long as I take the drug. If Steven never does work up the nerve to ask me to bring her back, he'll wish he had done so, but it doesn't matter because I know that I won't give it to her even if he asks.

It is this thought that keeps him alive, however. I am holding the key to his wife's survival.

He no longer sees me as the monster I have been portrayed to be. He has grown to stop believing in what others have to say, instead, he realizes he must learn from his own experiences. It is why he left for Horizon to begin with. I squeeze my eyes shut and wish for the Bloodleaf to stop.

"Steve?"

"Yeah, Mike?"

"Do you have any food? I'm dizzy."

"Hold on, man."

Steven reaches under a jacket I assume belongs to Masum. He pulls out a paper bag from one of the fast food restaurants on the ship.

"Do you want roast beef or a... chicken sandwich?"

"Chicken."

"You got it, sir."

I reach over and take the wrapped sandwich.

"Masum had a sack of these with him. He said he was with a buddy who worked on the ship before they took a nap, or had fallen asleep, or whatever. Small favors, you know?"

I nod and eat the sandwich. It's old and good.

I lie back against the side of the inflated raft and try to relax despite the unpredictable movements of the ocean. Eventually, I fell asleep, as Steven suggested, with nothing else to do. The sun harmlessly beat down on my drug-infused skin. My body would heal itself quickly after dosing but it would soon taper off. In a few days, I would start to die, again.

I slept and in my dream, I was trapped in ice. An eye was watching me through a crack in the ice, a tiny flicker of light shining through to warm my soul. I was cold and alone. The eye was the only breath I took in as the ice tore into my flesh and heart and the wind rushed in to fill the void burning off my block of ice. The eye pierced through the crack to reveal me inside, to reveal what was hidden within, and all that was around me spread out further and farther. I went deeper inside, riding the gaze to the middle of the destination, myself. The ice spread out from me as I remained encased.

Here I am again. Here we are again. There you are, further away than ever before and I am in a pain that you won't know.

I can feel nothing further. I can go no deeper as I spread eternity out before me. It seems as if only I could become smaller, that gaze goes deeper into me and moves farther away from me, and I awake.

I awake out of a dream I did not understand, washed up alongside a beach.

Avalon is a small island. Nothing but bleached and tanned sand, grass and rock, and a jut of a hill that rises in the middle. The gateway was visible ahead. I'd seen it many times.

"Stacie. Stacie wake up, honey, please!" Steven said, pulling his wife up from the floor of the raft. I look over and see Masum waking.

"Are we here?" Masum asks.

"Yes." We look at each other, knowing where *here* is.

Steven desperately prods his wife trying to wake her.

"Good," Masum says. He hops out of the raft onto the sand and turns to look at me. "It is good to see you again, Michael."

"It's good to see you, Masum. How is Allah today?" This is part of a well-meant joke I have with Masum, to which he answers honestly and truthfully, as he sees it. He knows I do not believe in a God, judging by the terrible atrocities committed by people in the name of the absolute confusion of being alive.

"Allah is merciful. There is no god except for Allah, and Muhammad was the messenger of Allah," he informs me, again.

"Thank you for the sandwiches, Masum."

"You ate them? Alhamdulillah. I did not expect to see you alive again and it was by the mercy of God we are here at all."

"It may be so, Masum." Though I don't believe this, I understand he does and he speaks from kindness.

"I see you standing here, Michael. You cannot tell me I don't see this, that we are not alive, and we have made it to where we needed to go."

"You are kind, Masum."

Steven's wife, Stacie, rouses and tries to sit up. He puts the canteen to her mouth and tries to help her drink, holding her head up. "Please, honey." His words are calm and pleading. She chokes and inhales forcefully, her face sunburned and peeling. She sputters and weakly sits back in the life raft as Steven kneels in the sand.

"Oh God, Steven. Where are we?" she says looking around in confusion.

"We're at the island, honey. We made it." Wrapping his arms around her, he presses his forehead to hers. Looking into her eyes, tears stream down his burned and cracked face. Kissing her lips, he sobs.

"I don't think I can get up, Steven."

"Try, honey, you can try. Please."

She turns onto her knees and tries to push herself to her feet and falls. Steven catches her as she clings to his shirt and leans against him. He looks at Masum and I.

"Can you help us?"

Masum says, "I can help her."

"Are you trying to go through the gateway?" I ask, grateful the Bloodleaf had worn off while I slept. I didn't need to take any, and I wouldn't wish to see the death bellowing from their hearts.

"Yes, please, help me get her through."

"Alright. There are people on the other side who will be able to help you. I can show you how to get through the gateway. There's a path nearby that will take us to the top of the hill."

With Steven's help, Stacie stumbles out of the raft and over to the grass beyond the sand and sits down. She puts a hand to her face. "Can I have some water?"

"Finish it," Steven says and holds out the canteen.

She wipes her hands on her pants and takes the water. We watch as she tips it back, then pours the rest over her hands and face.

"Where is the path, Michael?" asks Steven.

I look at what I could see of the gateway on the rise ahead. "We go around this hill. It shouldn't be far."

Steven kneels down with his wife and tries to help her up to her feet. Masum looks above the rise to the part of the gateway peeking out over the edge of the hill.

"Is that a statue of a woman?" he asks.

"Yes," I tell him, familiar with the statues.

He sighs. "I will have to study the island for a good while. It's a very special honor. I'm concerned I've lost my supplies."

I reach into my satchel and carefully sift through the bottom until I find a stem. I place it in my mouth and chew lightly as I remember all the other times I'd been on the island before this started. Masum looks down and walks over towards Steven and Stacie. He helps Steven lift Stacie to her feet and the two men begin walking with her. A stem will not dose me and I feel as if I have two more days left in my body.

The sand surrounding the hill sparkles, littered with bits of waterworn branches and other debris. The plants are long and green, as they've always been. I still wonder how life makes it to islands like these. I suppose wherever there is sun and water, there is food, and where there is food, there is life. The island is beautiful, lush and desolate. It always was under a Dreamer's influence, I'd never seen it any other way. We started to walk and I describe to the others what they will see.

"The gateway is three figures, or statues, at the top of the hill, in a clearing. They're supposed to be around twenty feet tall or so. One statue is of a man made of a brown rock with dense moss covering him. He has a stone knife on his hip. The one you can see now is the woman. They stand and make a triangle, each hand faces a statue to its left and right. The path will lead up in between the man and the woman."

Avalon was a small island, I cannot remember the exact size, but it's about a mile. There is not much space on the island and the hill and gateway are its primary feature. Steven spots the path leading up between the male and female figure and we start walking towards it.

"The woman is black stone?" Masum asks.

"Yes," I say, nodding my agreement. "She has rings and necklaces and her veins are gold running through the rock." We begin climbing up the path.

"You said there were three figures?" Steven says.

"Yeah, there's a third. It's supposed to be some type of metal or element. It's a silver color, but part of the figure has been destroyed, no one knows what exactly it is, but it seems to have arms and legs."

Walking up the path, we start to hear what sounds like scrapes and thuds coming from up ahead. Fear splashes through my stomach and I feel a blackness welling up behind my eyes, a tight ink that pours into my mind and strains my muscles.

"She will never make it through the gateway, Tyron! She will die here, she will rot and we will feed," a loud, hissing voice cried from the sky.

Masum let out a shout and pointed upward. In the sky, a large falcon-like creature, golden white, with a long arched neck stretches its wings widely and rises into the air, hurtling after the voice.

"You are a vile creature, Sar! I have fought you for a thousand ages. I feel no brief scuttle over the mortal remains of flesh should bother you or I!" As the large white falcon-drake speaks, its golden beak and claws gleam metallically in the sun, it dives towards the ground with a screech and there are more scraping sounds from the rise up ahead.

"You believe yourself so noble and virtuous, Tyron, yet you know, as well as I, you will pick her bones clean before I am even done cleaning the blood from my feathers, yes?"

"Michael, what's going on? What is this?" Steven shouts, frightened.

"I don't know, Steven, you know as much as I do. The gateway is supposed to make thoughts appear, but there's always been a Dreamer present whenever I've been here. I've never seen this."

"What the hell are you talking about? Are you talking about the crew on the ship?" he asks.

"Yes, I thought our Dreamer was near us somehow. I thought that's how we arrived at the island safely. I don't understand what is going on or what we are supposed to do."

Another large and black creature resembling the first one settled down in front of us. I clutch at my satchel and step back. Masum and Steven hold Stacie, our hackles rise.

"You see, Tyron? They are mortals, they cower in fear of something alive itself, they are no more worthy to fly and breathe as any other beast on which we feast."

The creature, Sar, the large, black falcon-drake spread its wings and preened its feathers in front of us. Each feather smoldered at the end and ashes fall to the ground as they burn. Tyron, the white one, with a gold metal beak and claws, settles beside Sar and tucks his wings in.

"Sar, you are gluttonous and you view these creatures as a meal and nothing more."

Sar raises his head high on his serpentine neck and lets out a burst of laughter. It sounds like a forest of birds taking flight. Masum quickly pulls Stacie away as Steven lets her go, falling to the ground in fear. Sar cranes his neck towards Steven, who stumbles and scrambles backward trying to find a place to hide himself. Sar closes an eye, in his other eye, his yellow iris reflects the light of the sun as his pupil dilates vertically.

Leaning down, inches from Steven's face, he asks, "Do you remember Melody, Steven? Do you remember how she laughed when you told her you wished you could make someone laugh again? That two years with your wife had proven to be more than your young mind could bear and you were lucky to have not birthed a child? You are weak and guilty, yes?"

Steven clawed at the ground around him, stammering, unable to form any words.

"Do not listen to his insolence, mortals. Sar bleeds fire, his veins course with the jealousy of death. It is why he chases me so," Tyron says in soothing tones, "He will cause you no harm."

Steven's face turned from fear to mottled rage. Seemingly from nowhere, a blade appears in his hand and he stabs it into the yellowed eye in front of him. The black monster whips its head to the side and lunges upwards, taking off into the sky.

"You feel wisely, mortal," Tyron says before taking flight after Sar, bellowing in triumph. Steven stands up and faces us, fighting for the control he lost only moments ago. "Let's go!" Steven yells fiercely. I start to walk towards the gateway and Masum helps Stacie to her feet. She pauses and hunches over.

"Steven, I don't think I can make it, let me lie down awhile, please!"

Steven gestures frantically. "No! Did you see that thing? It was going to kill us! We have to leave now!"

Forcing herself up, she yells back, "I don't want to go to Horizon! I want to go home, I want to stay here!" Tears falling down her face, she drops to the ground. Reaching down, Steven grabs her hand and pulls her towards him. Looking bewildered,

Masum steps backwards. I reflexively reach into my satchel and stop as I think better of it.

Turning toward me, Steven asks, "How do we get through the gateway, Michael?"

I pause for a moment. "The way we've done it is for any man to place their hand on the male statue's hand that is leading to the silver figure. You hold it until it feels warm, then walk to the silver figure, grasp its hand, and you will be in Horizon."

"What do the women do?" Steven asks.

"They do the same thing, it's just with the statue of the woman."

Steven turns and looks at his wife and says, "Honey, you have to go, you won't survive out here and we don't know if those-- things might come back."

Stacie's eyes flash and her face is fearful. She looks up into Steven's eyes and I watch as she clenches her teeth. They share a long look and then she looks away. "Okay," she says.

"Here," Steven says. He leads Stacie over to the black figure and places Stacie's hand on the figure's own. Though the statue stands much taller than all of us, its arms are down and fingers outspread. Masum looks up in wonder.

"Is it working?" Steven asks.

"I think, a little, yes," she says.

"How long does she wait?" Steven asks me.

"Not very long," I say.

"Alright," she says. She closes her eyes and takes a deep breath. A few seconds pass and she says, "I think it's alright now."

"Okay, just walk over to the silver statue and touch its hand, the one on the female side," I say.

"Okay," she says. She looks at the silver statue, then trembles and shudders.

"Will she be alright?" Steven asks me.

"Yes, she should be. There's a safe house close to the gateway. You'll want to head in the direction the silver statue is facing away from, someone should see you."

Stacie walks over and touches the silver statue's right hand. She breathes in and says suddenly "Oh God, I didn't know," and she's gone. Masum moans and turns away from us.

"Alright, Steven. You'll go to the moss-covered statue and grasp its hand until it feels warm, then touch the silver statue's hand on the other side."

Steven looks at the moss covered rock of the male figure. "Thank you, Michael, I won't forget this."

"Don't worry about it," I say.

Steven walks up to the male statue and places his hand in its rock-hewn fingers. The moss trails up its arm and covers its chest, head, and legs. The knife at its hip is simple in design, a stone wedge hanging from its waist.

"Just wait until you feel your hand get warm," I say to him.

He looks back at Masum and I. "I never did anything with that woman."

"What?"

"Melody. I never did anything with her. I only talked with her for a few weeks."

He sighs and walks over to the silver statue. Its face is broken off, flat, and a deep crack runs through the main part of the figure. Even though it is faceless, it holds its hands out all the same.

"You don't have much time," I say.

Steven nods, and walks over and places his hand on the outstretched palm of the silver metal statue, breathes sharply, and disappears.

Masum prays in Arabic. I look up at the sky and wonder when I will die.

CHAPTER 3

"Will you be going through the gateway, Michael?"

"Will you, Masum?"

Looking at the area around, he shrugs, "I want to study the island for a bit, but I don't have my supplies, they were on the ship."

He looks at me and cocks his head, "The man who would have paid my commission was on the boat, so I don't know if the job is to be done. I don't know if I go through the gateway that there will be anything for me. I will wait. If I go with you, they might arrest me," he says and lightly chuckles.

"I gathered up all of the plants I had and put them in this satchel," I replied, patting my bag.

"How much do you have?"

"I counted almost 2,000 leaves. It's over 300 years."

"So you can live for 300 years with what you have in your bag?" He looks surprised.

"Yeah, it was everything I had."

He thinks for a moment. "When a ship comes, can you leave and go back, do you know?" he inquires.

Thinking back to the time before I was arrested, I say, "They'll find me. A man who doesn't age and never dies can't stay hidden. Besides, my face has already been seen everywhere."

"Will you wait with me on the island?" He looks at me intently.

"With you, Masum?" I grin.

"Yes, with me, Michael. We can make ourselves a home here in the trees and welcome new people to Horizon. We can say 'Welcome to the land of plenty! Welcome to an infinite majesty waiting to be yours!'"

"Ha. I could dance and bang rocks together. We could collect tips."

"Now you are thinking, Michael! Allah is merciful, as I have told you. You have nothing to fear. He is with all things beautiful and good."

I think of the terrible tragedy my life was becoming.

"Yeah," I say.

I turn and look out over the sand into the ocean. Eventually, we find our way back to the gateway and Masum sits and begins studying the designs on the female statue. He traces his fingers over the gold veins running through the black stone.

I look at him and find myself saying, suddenly, "I want to die, Masum. I don't want to be alive anymore."

Masum turns to look at me. "I understand what you are saying, Michael. Maybe if you go to Horizon, you can be free of your struggles."

I look at the statues in front of us, at the male figure, a sandy brown with green moss, then at the silver statue which was unrecognizable as a man or woman. The female statue is beautiful, her back is arched, her chin high and inviting. Nothing was waiting for me but judgment and conviction on the other side of the gateway, confining me further in this imprisoned life, only now the prison will be on the outside as well as the inside.

"I believe your plant is a good thing, Michael. I have heard it brings a man back to life from the jaws of death. I have heard you say you will live a hundred years and more. What can be good but that? To live and breathe and marvel at the beauty around you and speak of it to others." He reached a hand to the sky trying to contain his excitement.

"That's what makes you a good artist, Masum," I say.

"I am not an artist. I have a talent with paints, and I am lucky to use them. I see what you do is beautiful, Michael. I can find no fault with you."

I can find everything wrong with me. "Do you want to take the Bloodleaf, Masum? I don't know when the next ship will appear. I don't believe there is anything to eat on the island. You would have to go through with me if you want to live. I can give you the plant, I can leave you with some, if you want to stay here," I say.

His eyes widened. "No, Michael, although I do appreciate you, I will stay here. I believe Allah will see me through."

"Okay," I say, and it begins to rain. It falls heavy, like a curtain in the air. We get wet, but it does not linger on our bodies. It feels as if the water falls through our skin.

"I let the Dreamer free, Masum. The Dreamer on the ship," I confess, stumbling over the words.

"She is the one that protects us?"

"Yes," I look into the sky. "I believe she is crying."

I turn to leave and start walking down the path. The rain is soft like wool and I try to come to terms with the thought of walking through the gateway, either now, or before the next ship arrives. I didn't know what was going to happen but I knew there was nowhere to save my life.

I want to die, every possible path leads to it, and yet I'm afraid.

At the trial, I can tell everyone what a terrible thing we are, what tragic consequences we bring, alive in this world or another, but in the end, I know I will not even do this. I cannot look someone in the eye and tell them what a tragic thing it is to be alive. I will cower out, I will take my punishment and they will keep me alive for as long as they can. Over three hundred years on what is in my bag. Longer, when they find Bloodleaf themselves, as it's only a matter of time.

I was the first to open Pandora's box and I was cruel to brandish its weapon, and it is too late now. The wound is stabbed into the Earth and I can't see or understand the consequences. I believed it was good to hear the thoughts of others. I thought it right to live forever, but it is a terrible pain.

Every person I have given the plant to is doomed, because like me, they won't die. Over time, they will realize what monsters they are to the innocent. Eventually, they will find themselves in a prison of their never-ending life.

No matter what time brings, their only recourse will be the threat of a terrible and painful death lurking in the shadows, each and every day they live. It is right that I go through the gateway, and they will find me, unless I stop taking the plant, here and now, and die in a day or so.

The rain passes by and I walk and look out at the sun as it is setting. I look at its red and golden hue, the sky is pale pink and red. The warmth of the sun reaches towards me and warms my face, faintly, and the air is cold. I kneel in the sand and I think of my own death. I'm too afraid to die.

Masum yells at me from the top of the hill. "Michael! Michael! Look!" he yells.

I turn to look at him and he is pointing up in the sky. In the distance, I see a helicopter making its way towards the island.

"You said the gateway makes dreams come true, Michael! I guess you didn't really want to die, my friend!"

I look up at the helicopter as it's getting closer. "Do we make a fire, Masum? How do they know to see us?" I yell back at him.

He starts running down the path. "They are here for you, Michael. You will see!"

I think and then suddenly panic as I realize someone might be making sure I had made it through the gateway. I run to a dense overgrowth on the side of the hill. "Tell them I died on the ship, Masum! Tell them I've died and this will stop! They will rescue you, I will try to go to New Civ and find a way to live!"

"You want me to lie to them, Michael?" he shouts, taken aback.

"Yes! Lie! Tell them you saw my body floating in the water. Tell them I was skewered with a metal pole and all of my Bloodleaf fell into the ocean and is lost forever. Tell them I went painfully, and I begged for help-- no, no, tell them people tried to help me and I said 'No! Let me die because I am a cruel monster and it is too painful to live!' Tell them this and save my life, Masum!"

He stands back as the helicopter comes closer to the island.

It begins its descent onto the sand and the grass nearby is blown back in a circular pattern. I crouch lower and Masum braces himself against the force of the helicopter landing.

The blades come to a stop and a door in the side opens. Three men step out and one of them raises a rifle at Masum. Through the brush and branches, I see a figure behind the two armed men speak, his voice is faint but carries. "We're looking for Michael Janice. The ship that was wrecked in the ocean, he was supposed to be on it. We saw him here, where is he?"

Masum spreads his hands out and pauses. "I don't see him, do you see him?"

The men look around and then back at Masum.

"Do you know where he is?" The man behind the two in front asks.

Masum stammers and looks down at the ground. "I did not see the man you are talking about." I see the same look on his face as when I had asked him if he wanted the Bloodleaf.

The man briefly places his hand on the shoulder of one of the men standing in front of him and a rifle fires soon after. Masum falls to the ground. The armed man steps over his body and I turn away as he fires again.

"Michael! We know you're on the island!"

I turn back and see the man quietly speak to the other two. He points, then they nod and go separate directions.

"And don't try anything funny. I have a psychologist with me who is sensitive to this sort of thing. I pay her good money."

I ransack my mind.

"Do you remember a gentleman by the name of Paul Reely, Michael? He's the one you first gave that plant of yours to, what is it, five years ago now? You started your business with him, thought you'd cure the world of its ills?"

Paul Reely. I had not seen Paul in over a year. The media had also mentioned his name and there had been court proceedings and government agencies asking for information and looking for him.

"He's dead, Michael. They found his body. What was left of it." He pauses. "Glad I caught up with you."

I stiffen as I feel something metal pushing firmly against my back.

"Heat sensor, motherfucker."

I turn to look at the man as a boot kicks me in the head. I try to lift myself up, but my muscles are dead. He rears his arms up and slams the butt of his rifle down and I am powerless.

"You move again, motherfucker, and I'll break it in."

The man on the beach yells out, "Ahh, good. You found him! Bring him here, sir. Does he have a bag, or a suitcase?"

"He's got a purse, sir, it looks pretty full."

"Grab it," the man on the beach says.

Quivering, I watch the man with the gun take my open satchel and throw it behind him. Some of the dried leaves fall out. I yell out with a terror I don't understand and try to lunge for the bag as the man pushes me back down on the ground with his foot.

"You don't do that," he says.

"Tie him up," says the man on the beach.

I lay on the ground, dirt sticking to my face and bleeding. I'm pulled roughly onto my side. My hands are forcefully pulled behind me and my wrists are tied together quickly. The other person who had been looking for me arrives. My feet are tied and I am hoisted by my shoulders out onto the beach.

"Do you have the bag?" the man says to the ones holding me.

"Yeah, some of the shit in it fell out, though," I hear the man who had attacked me say.

"That's okay. It won't matter much." The man looks at me, "My wife has taken a liking to this plant. I want to know how you grow it."

My eyes are open and blood is getting into them. I'm blinking back stinging tears and trying not to gasp and choke.

"Let me see the bag," he says. I hear as the satchel is opened and his hands sift through it.

"Watch this, gentlemen." He tears off a bit of a dried leaf and places it on my tongue.

I do my best to spit it out.

The man's voice sounds strained. "Take the plant, Michael. I've seen what it does."

I lift my head up and my skull is ringing. The brightness of what is left of the sunlight is causing my skull to ring and I am trying to find warmth. "I don't care."

I will die in two days. The man closes the satchel. "Get him inside."

The two men with rifles roughly pull me into the helicopter and drop me on the floor. I hear a woman seated towards the front turn and gasp.

"What did you do to him? Is he going to tell you how to grow the plant?" she says loudly.

The man with the satchel looks at her, "He won't eat it."

"What about your wife?"

I hear the satchel land in a seat. "That's enough for her to live on while I get this figured out."

He looks at the pilot and says, "Take us up, take us back to the ship. We need to get back. Hurry."

I hear the blades of the helicopter start to spin and I suddenly feel very tired.

"What's in the bag, sir?" one of the armed men asks.

The man who tried to give me the plant is older, his hair is white and neatly combed, his eyes blue, he wears yellow.

"Did I ask you to do or say anything?" the blue-eyed man says.

The man with the gun, who had hit my skull with the butt of his rifle, quiets down.

"Michael, I want you to know that I am going to take off every last bit of flesh from your body until you tell me how to grow this plant," Blue-eyes tells me.

I say nothing and I'm staring at the lines on the floor spreading out from the side of my face as the helicopter begins to vibrate. I imagine the lines are a maze and a little boy, who is me, runs through the lines, jumping and shouting wildly every time the line ends or takes a turn.

The man with the gun kicks me in the stomach and I curl back. "Mr. Johnson asked you a question."

Little me runs back and forth until he gets close to my face and stares at my eyeball in front of him, marveling at how big it is. He looks at himself in its reflection, patting down his wild hair. I grin, secretly.

The man kicks me in the stomach again. I feel like I will vomit.

"Marcus, you are singly the stupidest man I have ever had on a payroll, do you know that?" I hear Marcus get the back of his head slapped. Blue-eyes walks towards me, bends down and looks me in the swollen eye. My brow furrows and I clench my teeth, afraid.

"Michael, if you think for one moment I'm going to let you die before I'm done with you, you had better understand that I won't," he shouts as the noise in the helicopter increases.

The little boy, who is me, spins in a circle with his arms outstretched. He dances, foot to foot, raising his head back.

"I don't care," I mumble.

He leans closer and places a hand behind his ear.

"What?" he says.

I feel my front teeth loosen with my tongue. I carefully clean the blood from my lips, avoiding my front teeth, so as not to lose them. I say again, "I don't care."

He leans down and I feel his breath on my ear. I smell sandalwood cologne and blood.

"You better fucking care, you little prick, because I will shove this goddamned plant up your ass as I am personally peeling your skin from your body, do you understand? You think you don't care? I know pieces of shit like you. You do care. You think you can sit here and tell me you don't care, now?"

I see the blue eyed, white haired man named Johnson grin and the little boy in the maze looks up at his face and smiles, waving at him.

"I'll tell you something, Michael, listen close," Blue-eyes says.

He places his mouth right next to my ear and I hear the saliva on his lips and tongue.

"I," he whispers, "don't care."

Painfully, I close my eyes as he gets up. I hear the woman in the front say "Why don't you just give him the plant? I can't bear to look at him."

"Let the little prick suffer. Like he said, he's gonna die. Who cares? We've got the plant. Don't worry, he won't die. Neither will Wendy."

"You know, your wife is revealing a deep neurosis as she continues to take this drug, David," the woman says.

"Do you think I don't know that? I am paying for those clothes you wear and you think I don't know my wife is a fucking lunatic?" The voices sound like they are coming from a loudspeaker inside the helicopter now.

The woman makes a 'tsk' sound with her tongue. I hear this. "Why do you think money will solve everything, David?"

"It doesn't solve everything. You can't even figure out something that I'm paying you to figure out, you're the one asking me questions and I already know my wife is a fucking lunatic. I've got a question for you, Dr. Lockard," he says with emphasis, "At what point do you stop wasting my money and time?"

She breathes in heavily and it feels like the air is sucked out of the helicopter. I continue staring at the floor and I see a small campfire appear between some of the lines. The little boy puts a hand to his ear and I smile weakly as he hears the crackle and burn.

His mouth opens widely and a look of excitement and anticipation appears in his eyes as he scrambles up the side of the line wall, out of the maze and on to the flat ground. He raises his hands joyfully as he sees the fire and runs to it. He begins to dance around the fire.

I feel my neck and shoulders loosen a little as a wave of pain from a bruise on my face courses through my blood. I smile inwardly and pray for rain with him. The little boy bears his chest and looks at me proudly. He breathes in deeply through his nostrils. He jumps in the air and runs around with his arms outstretched. He is an airplane, now.

"What are you laughing at, fucker?" Marcus says to me.

I ignore him and watch the little boy, who is me, lie down in front of the fire. I see little stars appear in the sky above him, and a moon is out, crescent, with a wisp of cloud across it. I see a mountain off in the distance and a coyote howls. The little boy shivers in his sleep. I feel sad for the little boy.

Marcus looks at me again and says, "What the fuck are you laughing at, prick?"

"I am laughing at myself." My teeth are loose.

"You better shut the fuck up, or I'll kick your ass, asshole."

I hear Blue-eyes say, "Marcus, would you like a tea set and a teddy bear or two so you can have a little tea party with your new best friend?"

I say nothing.

Time passes, and the helicopter continues its slow vibration. I look out over the little boy, into the night, watching over and protecting him. Every now and then, a coyote will come down from the mountains and sniff around the light from the campfire, but I glare at it and it skulks off. One time I blew at one from my mouth, and it ran scampering with its tail between its legs. The little boy turns over in his sleep and sighs.

At one point I hear Johnson ask the pilot how long it would be until we arrived at our destination. The pilot said something, but the noise muffled his response.

I close my eyes for a bit as the little moon sets, confident the boy will be alright for a small while, and think of nothing at all. Inside my mind is black and blank, with colors and fractals appearing here and there. I rest.

After a bit, I feel the pressure in the helicopter shift suddenly and we sway. We seem to right ourselves and nothing else happens for a while. I open my eyes and see a little girl with black hair, dark skin, and a splash of freckles across her face lying next to the boy, who is me. She wears a green frock and she sleeps with her arms to her sides, her fists clenched and her eyes closed.

The boy is curled on his side with his hands under his head and his feet tucked under himself. Her face is calm as she sleeps. It is dark in the cabin, the sun has set, and it is night.

Everyone is quiet and calm.

I can see a soft glow coming from the front, and a few scattered lights inside the cabin. I start to feel the blood and sweat on my face and realize I had slept, briefly. I stir and tilt my head slightly, my neck aches and feels bruised and my face is tender and swollen. I can't open my right eye, and I blink out tears from it every now and then.

"I'll take the plant," I say, loudly. No one responds.

"I will take the plant. I will take the Bloodleaf," I say louder this time, trying not to tremble. I hear faint snoring.

"Mr. Johnson?" I hear nothing.

"David?" I say, trying again. After a moment, I hear the rustle of his movement.

"What is it, Michael?" he asks.

"I'll take the Bloodleaf. I'll tell you how to grow the plant."

"I know," he says.

"I'll take it now. Please let me have it."

"No," he says.

It remains quiet and after a while, I feel the helicopter start to land.

CHAPTER 4

I awake in a guest room in a plantation in what was still South America. I can hear voices through the door. It's a news reporter speaking about my apparent death. I look around the room. I'm lying on a comfortable mattress with threaded sheets and multiple pillows. The curtains around the window are drawn back and letting in the high noon sun spill in its light.

The news speaks about the loss of the ship Odyssey, and the deaths of hundreds of passengers, many respected individuals. The world is beset with shock and emotion, faced with the first significant, impacting development to have taken place in the Horizon saga since my apprehension.

I am dead at least, it is assumed. The incident's precipitation is speculated and it is thrown around as to whether or not my ability for mental manipulation played any involvement in the disaster.

Since everyone knows the area surrounding the gateway manifests thoughts, it is believed I had somehow taken mind control of the Dreamer and jeopardized the safety of the other passengers and was instrumental in the tragedy. The bodies that were recovered were broken, burned and had otherwise suffered physical carnage. The Dreamer's capsule was recovered and found empty and further investigations could not be conducted without another Dreamer present. The travel ship, Gratuity, whose Dreamer was recovering from a prior drug stasis, would be available to travel in less than a week.

A GSS official was heard after the report. He stated the Odyssey shipwreck was a terrible tragedy and in the interest of global security, the remaining members of what was known as "The Circle" must be apprehended. He stated the ringleader, Paul Reely, was found dead and they would continue to seek the remaining members of the cult.

"How many members of the Circle are left?" I hear through the door. I hear the GSS official's grave and somber voice again.

"It's not known at this time. The drug was not found in Paul Reely's possession and we have no knowledge of how many people Michael Janice or Paul Reely may have made addicts."

"Can conventional weapons stop them?"

"Yes. Although their mental manipulation limits are unknown, we are aware that without the plant, the Circle cannot recover from physical harm. We ask if you suspect an individual you may know to be an addict to immediately contact local authorities who will divert the information to the appropriate channels. Your identity and any information will remain protected."

"Dr. Tatsumi, sir, what impact do you believe the Odyssey massacre will have on the Circle?"

"We believe that those addicted to the drug will seek help and notify their local governments so that treatment and rehabilitation can begin. We understand those with the addiction may not want to reveal themselves for fear of condemnation. Our utmost concern is treating them and we expect full cooperation. No further questions at this time, please."

"Alright, that was Dr. Harold Tatsumi of GSS in London. Joining us via satellite we have two distinguished members of global discourse. I'd like to introduce Mr. Karl Ramis, bestselling author of In Search of the Hidden Vista. How are you, Mr. Ramis?"

"I'm fine, Betsy, how are you today?"

"I'm great, as always, thank you. I see you're wearing a purple tie, are you showing support for National Women's Month, Karl?"

"Haha, no, I like the color purple." I hear a smattering of laughter and applause.

"Also with us, we have the co-founder of HPR, Dr. Steven Calden. Dr. Steven, how are you today?"

"Great, great, doing fine, Betsy. The weather here is wonderful in Minnesota."

"That's wonderful, Dr. Calden. Now, Mr. Ramis, you have publicly stated you oppose the measures that Dr. Calden and 'Horizon Policy Reform' reflect, is that correct?"

"Not entirely, Betsy. I am more for a careful consideration of the philosophical and ethical questions brought on by a living existence with an infinite dimension. I do not directly oppose HPR as an entity or agency."

"Dr. Calden?"

"Thanks, Betsy, and I just want to say, Karl, that I haven't personally read your book, but I hear it offers astounding insights into the human perspective."

"Thank you, Steven, those are kind words."

"Now, as anyone may or may not be aware, The Horizon Policy Reform action was not put together by a hastily cobbled arm of the wealthy aristocrats in society as it's so often been labeled. The actions of HPR are, for one, to support the beliefs that the tenets of a liberated democracy support the views of Horizon as a lush and fertile landscape and the impact of its existence should be handled responsibly by elected representatives."

"Mr. Ramis?"

"Betsy, I agree that Horizon and its ramifications should be handled responsibly. However, I believe this responsibility can and should be handled by the population and not represented by policies established by an organization intent on governing a new world."

"Mr. Ramis, you're an American, correct?" I hear the voice of Dr. Calden say.

"You know I am, Dr. Calden."

"What is wrong with government representation? I'm assuming you don't support the anarchistic viewpoints of several individuals who tout an anti-government mindset?"

"No, Dr. Calden, I simply believe that humanity ought to hold the reins of a new world collectively and not through a fabricated social construct that you propose."

"Mr. Ramis, you are aware that we are live?"

"Indeed, I am, Dr. Calden."

"Are you accusing the American government of being a fabricated social construct?"

"No, Dr. Calden, I am merely suggesting that we take foresight and responsible philosophical and ethical questioning as a spearhead to Horizon as a population and not create a small group of people as the sole carriers of those responsibilities."

"Mr. Ramis--"

The voices stopped. I looked at the dresser and my clothes from yesterday were neatly washed, pressed and folded on the top. I'd been taken to the room in the early morning before the sun had risen. I was stripped and my face was gone over with a damp cloth and I slept. I hadn't showered, my skin was gritty against the sheets, though I'd had the opportunity to dose before falling asleep. My satchel was left behind on top of the dresser next to the clothing.

I hear a knock at the door.

"*Mr. Yanice? Mr. Yanice, sir?*"

"Yes?" I say alarmed.

"Dr. Lockard would like to see you."

The voice belonged to the woman who had taken care of me in the middle of the night.

I dressed and opened the door to a middle-aged South American woman with black hair and dark complexion wearing an apron. She addresses my chest.

"She is this way, please," she says, pointing off towards some unknown location.

I turned towards the dresser and picked up my satchel. I follow the maid and we walk by somber brown and black walls and white unlabeled doors.

"What is your name, *Señora*?" I ask. "*¿Còmo te llamas?*" She was walking quickly.

"Oh," she says without turning and shakes her head.

At the end of the hallway, she holds out her hand to the door on the right and leaves me standing there alone to knock on my own. I look back at her hurrying toward where I assumed the broadcast was from.

The door is much the same as mine and all the others with a glass etched door knob and brass door plate. I was surprised that I'd been led to the Doctor's guestroom. I knock.

"Come in, Michael."

I open the door into a large office. The desk in the center is solid and wood, with a gloss finish. The windows behind Dr. Lockard were wide and revealed a green landscape and blue sky. Other parts of the plantation could be seen in the distance. Several bookshelves lined the walls along with a vase and a few lamps.

Behind the desk, Dr. Lockard looks up behind round, antiquated eyeglasses. Her short, brown hair falls simply to her chin. She pulls a sleeve of her pale green blouse up to her elbow and indicates a chair in front of her.

"Sit down, please."

I sit down in the chair. She turns and bends to her left, reaching into a drawer in her desk. She pulls out a small packet of papers, stapled neatly in the corner.

"Mr. Johnson would like for me to give you a mental evaluation, Michael."

She picks up a pen and peers at the paper over her eyeglasses.

"What does he want to know?"

"He wants to know a little bit about your background. It's standard for anyone who begins working with him."

"Since when have I been working with him, or even wanted to work with him?" I said, somewhat incredulously considering how I had arrived here.

"I don't believe he's giving you a choice. It would be better if you answer truthfully and without any stress, so I can provide the best kind of feedback."

"Stress?" I say. I look blankly around the office and then back at Dr. Lockard. "Alright."

"How many brothers and sisters do you have, Michael?"

"None," I say. "I'm an only child."

"Are your parents alive?"

"Yes."

"What are their names?" she asks.

"I'm not comfortable giving you that information, but I'm sure you can find out."

"That's fine, Michael. How old are they?"

"My mother is 56, my father is 60."

She continues writing on the paper. "Are they separated? Married?" she asks.

"They're still married," I say.

"How long have they been married?"

I tried to remember their last anniversary. We hadn't spoken in over a year, but I remembered they met a few years before I was born.

"Twenty-seven years."

"They had only one son?"

I closed my eyes and tilted my head back. "I think my mother had gotten pregnant when I was young."

"They stopped trying to have children after that?" she asks.

"I guess so," I say, rubbing the back of my hand.

"Have you ever been in a long-term relationship, Michael? Did you have a high school sweetheart?"

I look at her blankly.

"Michael?"

I hold back vague frustration. "At 24, I dated a girl who worked on a Horizon travel ship with me."

"Did you kiss her?"

"What?"

"How close were you, Michael?"

I clear my throat.

"I'm just trying to reason out your attitude towards people who are close to you."

I breathe out. "I don't know," I say.

She writes again.

"How did you meet Paul Reely?"

I look at the vase against the wall to her right. It's white with ribbons of pink entwining it. "I met Paul Reely in middle school."

"So you two grew up together?"

"You could say that."

She flips through several pages of the packet and finishes writing.

"Alright, Michael. I believe you can eat lunch downstairs now. I'll call for you when I need you again."

I pause. "Why was I allowed to have the satchel back?"

"I don't know why David let you have the satchel back, Michael. I think he supports the power that individuals can attain for themselves. Maybe he wouldn't keep you from your own." She looks off for a moment.

I look down at my knees and rise out of the chair. I feel nothing.

"Thank you, Michael," she says, and turns back to her paperwork.

Walking out of the office, I look into my satchel and believe it to be lighter than it had been, but not considerably so. It looked like the mass of leaves had been shoved back into the bag. The smell wafted up to my nose, a bittersweet and sickly smell.

I look down the hallway as sunlight spills against the doors to the right from an opening in the hallway on the left, the stairs leading down to the front entrance.

The color of the hallway, brown and black, earthy colors, gave a feeling they were seeping into my mind through my eyes. It was comfortable and it pricked at my sense of being home, though I was sick to my stomach. I didn't want to be here, it was dangerous. I believed I had been welcomed into a viper's nest. The snakes slithered around my insides, squeezing with touch and contact, but no warmth, as they pulled me in through their ceaseless and undulating motions.

I walked to the staircase and took a step down. I looked ahead at the wide and multi-angled window above the main door. The sun shone brightly and the hills and trees went on in a way that let me know we were close to nowhere. We arrived by a small boat traveling upriver through the night. Avalon was off the coast of South America and we'd gone far inland. There were no clouds in the sky.

"*Mr. Yanice?*" A voice calls to me as I step off the staircase.

I turn and see the maid waiting for me with a smile on her

face. I had not seen this yet.

"Come and have lunch, *Mr. Yanice*. My husband, Emanuel, will eat with you."

She is noticeably more chipper.

"Thank you, *Señora*. What is your name?"

"Maria, *Mr. Yanice*."

"Michael."

Maria leads me through a door and down another hallway until we enter a room which turns out to be a screened-in outdoor patio. A wall of heat hits my face and my forehead breaks out in sweat. There are several cushioned chairs and a long table. Plants were seated in the corners and hung from the beams holding the top of the structure up. I see more of the hilly land traveling for what was probably miles.

"Please sit down, *Mr. Yanice*. I will bring lunch."

I sat down in a wicker chair to the right. Through another door, a man comes walking through. He is dark skinned and slightly sweaty as if he had been out in the sun. His eyes sweep the room as his head leans forward with a nervous energy, an eagerness that makes it seem as if he is looking for something.

He spies me and pulls a chair out from the table and straddles it facing me.

"Mr. Janice?" His accent is faint.

"Yes?" I say, cautiously.

He holds out a hand. "I'm Emanuel. I lived in the States for a while, how are you?"

I take his hand because it's offered. "I'm alright, Emanuel. How are you?" I say with no emphasis.

"Good, good! It's a hot day out today, and I like it!" he says.

"Yes, it is."

He hunches farther over the back of the chair and wipes his forehead, looking off to the side. He turns his gaze back to me. "You don't talk much, do you?"

"I'm not really too happy about being here, I don't have much to talk about."

He leans back and grins. "Hey, you'll like it here, don't even worry!" He leans forward and slaps me on the arm.

He continues looking around and rubs his hands together. "I

can't wait to eat, I'm starving."

I have no idea what is happening. I understand that David Johnson, who I assume owns this mansion and the land surrounding it, wants me to help him to grow Bloodleaf. Also, it seems his wife is addicted to the plant and I don't know if I've ever met her, nor where she is getting it from.

I am probably being offered a type of freedom in exchange for helping to grow the plant. Not only do I not know if I have a choice, I'm sickened by the fact that I would welcome the opportunity. I force the thoughts down and realize I am thought to be dead.

"So, that's the bag, huh?" Emanuel says. He's continuing to look around, although he's doing his best to hide it.

"I'm sorry?" I'm beginning to become terrified and it's blocking anything else I could be feeling.

Behind me, the door swings open and Maria is carrying in two plates of food. Emanuel leans back and grins widely, spreading his arms. "Finally," he says, and rubs his hands together.

Maria sets two plates down on the table and then some silverware. She leans over and kisses Emanuel on the cheek. She looks at me with her chin down and a red blush appears across her face. She turns and walks back through the door.

"Eat, man," Emanuel says, "I promise you it will be good." He takes a plate from the table and hands it to me, then hands me the silverware. Soon, the door opens again and Maria places two large glasses on the table that look filled with ice cubes and tea. She wipes her hands from the condensation and disappears back through the door.

"It's tea with brandy," Emanuel confides with a wink.

I look down at the plate and it smells wonderful. Grilled chicken breast and seasoned yellow rice with peppers and onions.

"Eat," he says, encouraging me by taking a bite.

I eat. I can go without food for long stretches of time, but I hadn't eaten much for several days. The flavors settle on my tongue and we chew silently.

"You know, Michael," Emanuel says as he reaches over for

his drink, "I'm pretty excited about you being here. A lot of people are happy about you being here." He sips and places the glass down and continues eating.

I pause and hold the plate out, looking out through the screen of the patio. "You knew I would be here?"

"Are you kidding? We didn't know you'd be here, but we knew how wonderful it would be. I still can't believe Mr. Johnson got you here. We're really excited."

I swallow and say, "Who's we?"

"The workers here. I help run them, you can look at it that way."

"What do you do?"

"We grow coca leaves, Michael. We process some of the leaves, too."

Anxiety sinks into my stomach and settles with the food. Somewhere outside I hear a lawnmower start.

"It's really something," he laughs. "The plant, you know? I mean, you live forever? You have to take it every three days?" He laughs again and makes a motion as if he is wiping a tear from his eye.

"We're going to grow it. Right here. We've got tons of land. I mean, it's really amazing."

The food loses its taste and it is an effort to swallow.

"They'll have to buy it, you know. All the time. We'll have to grow a lot. Eat up."

I try to stop the plate from shaking in my hand.

"Who wouldn't want to live for a really long time?" he says and makes a noncommittal shrug.

I look at him. "It's terrible," I say. I can not remember his name. "Death puts an end to life. Death is what gives life meaning. It's not something you just... It's not a decision you can just make."

"You did," he says. "Why are you talking about death, Michael? Why would anyone want to die? They won't have to worry about that and neither do you." He points at the plate. "Eat," he says. "No, that's a miserable way of looking at things." He finishes, takes a drink from his tea and slaps me on the arm again. "I've got to go, think about what I said, okay? Try not to worry so much, everything's going to be fine." He leaves out the door he came in.

There was no sense, in the end. There was no right inside of anyone. We would destroy the choices we needed to make. I'm left with a cold and artificial understanding instead. A white vase with a pink ribbon encircling it, a sterile and pointless example of nothing.

I place the plate on the table and still my hands as a bitterness runs through me and I am afraid. Someone was placing ether in front of my nose and mouth and all I could do was breathe deeply. I could blame no one any longer. I'd been looking for what was right and lost what I was looking for because it was never there. I was being given an opportunity to make others suffer as I was and no one believed it, and in fact, willingly denied it, in anticipation of having the drug themselves, or the benefit of it for themselves.

Keep talking, Michael.

Eat up, Michael.

I find myself at a dinner table, watching another play enacted by human beings fed up with anything, the useless drama of their own lives no longer exciting aside from what I possessed, how they could make their lives exciting with it and how to make it a part of their own. This was all in my own mind.

I hadn't made the decision to show them how to grow the plant and yet it already belonged to them. They were already extrapolating events far beyond their own understanding.

It proved to me we were all somehow sick inside, not sick with disease, or sick in the mind, but sick in the heart. We were bodies of rippling water and we shaped and formed whatever we could, including each other and ourselves. We chose our own reasons and we could not even know if we truly believed them.

It was not that there wasn't any reason or warmth throughout, it was that we had no ken or possession of it, save for what revealed itself through our own purposes, even if no one else could see it, even if it couldn't be shared, even if we had no idea why, and this was a terrible pain. How would it ever bring comfort? Even our own awareness constantly evaded us in an attempt to be free.

I had found something that would change this and shared it simply because I believed it to be the right thing to do.

Something in the plant heals your body, it shows you someone's mind and can show your mind to them, the things you or they can't express, the things you or they can't share, that you or I or anyone would not be alone with something if or when they chose not to be and could share something if they needed to but had no way to.

After Paul and I had eaten the plant together, before we knew what we knew, we had given it to some friends in our apartment.

That was when we found out you would rot and die if you didn't eat it again, otherwise you would live indefinitely.

I spent three weeks trying to come to a decision about showing how the plant was grown. I was never able to actually leave the plantation. I was given the satchel back because of how meaningless I was.

CHAPTER 5

"Michael?"

There are twelve oak trees in a meadow. It's going around. I can't stop it.

"Michael, stay with me."

I want to die. I don't want to be alive anymore.

"Michael, it's okay. I need you to concentrate on your name."

Please understand, he really only has his hands.

"Please, Michael, this is important. Can you feel my hand?"

What?

"Can you feel my hand, I'm holding yours."

I don't know where I am.

"Michael, what do you see?"

What? Who are you?

"What do you see, Michael? Where are you?"

I wish my head was burned and buried in salt. I wish I could breathe water and choke. I wish I had been anywhere but where I was.

"Some of us do."

"I don't think the plant will last through a dry season, though."

"It might."

"You said you grew it, right?"

"Yeah. Inside, though. Does it snow here?"

"No, it does get cold. I'm more concerned about drought."

"I don't think there's going to be anything to worry about," I said.

"What about any disease or insects? What do you know about it? I've only seen the plant I have," she said.

"It's strong." I hadn't yet told her how the plant was grown. This was why she wanted to come out here. Wendy didn't want to be around anyone else when we ate it. We would need to take it together for a new plant to take root.

"We'll do it right here, okay?" Wendy's red and loosely curled hair seemed auburn in the moonlight. Her eyes were a light brown, almost copper, and the ambient light traced her features and lithe frame.

"Yeah," I say. I place her plant down, it's pot quietly touching and firmly resting on the ground. She had one of the plants Paul and I had grown. When we found out I was going to be arrested, Paul had taken several and we had dried out the rest. Paul had always known me. Despite that, he tried to save people anyway. We decided I would be the one to start telling everyone about what we had.

Wendy bought her plant from Matthew Rindale, a friend of Paul's, confiding she spent quite a bit to have it.

It stood a little over two feet, it's center stalk was straight, the broad tear-drop shaped leaves spiraled upwards and were tightly packed together and it was still in the same pot Paul and I had grown it in.

"What do we do?" she asked.

"Do you have a knife or blade we can use?"

"I have a scalpel. It's clean." She pulls out folded white gauze from the pocket of her jacket.

"Okay, hold on." I bend down and sweep away debris from the rough earth with my fingers and wipe my hands on the fabric of my jeans.

"What we are going to do is cut a leaf from the plant as close to the stalk as we can, then place the stem into the ground. Hold on."

I look around until I find a rock and use it to tear up a patch of dirt until the soil is loose. Finished, I toss it back on to the ground and stand up again. The sound muffles and fades into the night.

"When you place the stem of a leaf into the soil, it needs blood to grow," I say.

Her lips part and her eyes narrow. Even in the pale light, I see the telltale signs of heat rise in her face. "Blood?"

"It needs blood from both of us after we've dosed. That's how the leaf will grow roots."

She looks to the side, thinking. Her lips are still parted and she moistens them with the tip of her tongue. She does this twice.

"Okay," she says. She reaches out a hand to touch my arm, then pulls it away and begins unwrapping the scalpel. She would never touch me again. "What happens when we both eat it?"

"We'll be able to see through each other's eyes," I had already told her this, but I'd come to realize Wendy needed simple truths, repeated, it was her manna.

"Alright," she turns towards the leaves circling the stalk and then back at me. "Can you do it?"

I take the scalpel from her hand and take a leaf from near the top and hold it steady with my left hand. Using my right to block the leaves surrounding it, holding the blade and handle in my fingertips, I deftly nick the stem going to the stalk and pull the leaf out. She places the gauze back into her pocket.

"We'll heal while we're bleeding, we'll have to hold the skin open," I say. Kneeling down, I place the stem of the leaf into the torn up ground and sweep the loose dirt into the center to prop the leaf up. I press the mound firmly together.

"Do we eat the leaves together?" she asks.

"We don't have to. We'll have about ten minutes, that's more than enough time. The more blood that runs into the ground, the larger the plant will grow."

"You go first," she says.

"Alright." I reach over to the plant and pull off another leaf.

"Do we need to eat the same leaf?"

"No," She'd already learned you didn't need to eat much of the plant.

She reaches down and pulls a leaf from the stalk. We are

standing still in the moonlight, and she holds the leaf tight in her trembling fingers. The trees are dark and I smell mist. I look at her, but I don't actually see anything.

"Are you okay?" she asks.

"Yes," I say. "No. It doesn't matter." I bend the leaf and bite down, chewing. The bitter taste waxes the roof of my mouth and tongue. My lips tremble and I swallow.

I look over at her again. "We need two blades. We have to do this together."

She looks at the mound with the leaf standing in it. "You go ahead. I'll follow." Her eyes focus on me and she is studying my features. I feel the Bloodleaf begin working its way through and I start to see a fiery sun blazing from her mind. There is no one else around in my range. The sun darkens and a red rain appears to surround us. I shudder. I don't understand.

I take the blade and press it into my arm below the wrist, pulling the blade towards the center of my body. The sun in her mind turns electric blue and seems to radiate through the darkness in the woods where we are. The pain is sharp and fades quickly as I lean over and hold the skin open with the scalpel, the blood twining down my wrist and hand, dripping on to the mound.

"Keep going," she encourages, watching me with wide eyes.

As I squeeze my fist tighter, more blood flows into the ground, and I cannot understand why I didn't ask her to bring a second blade. "We have to do this together," I say.

"It'll mix," she says. "I'll go over the top of it when you're done."

My skin is mostly healed and I pull the blade through it again. I look up at Wendy and her mind is poison. I see the gauze in her pocket and she pulls it out. I wait a little longer and then hand her the blade. She wipes it with the gauze, cleaning the grooves and edges, and I see that her name was Linda as a child.

She chose the name Wendy because she hadn't wanted anyone to know her. She once had another life and she knew more people as Wendy than she did as Linda. I am unable to tell what is happening to her. She had a plan and now I was a part of it. Spears erupted from the ground around her thoughts, bones caved in on themselves and we were burning in a desert sunlight again.

Taking off her jacket, she sits on the ground with her legs folded under herself, the blade in one hand, a leaf in another.

"I don't know what you can see, Michael, but don't worry," she says. Delicately, she lifts the leaf, and bites a piece off and chews. "It's all going to be alright. I know it will. That's why I'm here. I feel it."

I, myself, can see nothing but death in her mind. She swallows the juice from the leaf and I watch water pour over sand, evaporating. There is no sun now, but the desert is dry and hot.

She looks at me as the Bloodleaf takes effect. "You're not even afraid, Michael. You hate everyone. You hate the world?"

"You want it to die," she said, after a moment.

"I know," I say. "Paul knew, too."

"You don't even care, do you?" she asks.

"No, I don't. That's why I'm doing this."

The Bloodleaf in our bodies sang out and I looked through her eyes. I saw myself sitting in the dirt, my eyes were sad and my lips were parted. I was looking down at the leaf.

"I don't even care what happens anymore," I watched myself saying. "I just want it all to end."

She looks down at her arm and presses the blade to her skin. "Don't worry," she says. "It won't."

She watches through my eyes as the blood trails down her arm, into the soil, and she laughs without thinking for the first time in her life.

CHAPTER 6

Sitting down next to me on the patio, Maria asked, "Michael, why are you sad, always?" Placing a basket of warm biscuits on the table with a cloth covering them, she encouraged me to have one. She did not speak English well and was embarrassed by this. When she understood that I didn't judge her for it, she opened up. She didn't speak much, but unlike her parents, she was able to communicate with the people she worked for and that pleased her.

When I declined the biscuits, she grumbled and looked worried. "It's not sadness," I said. I made my decision with Wendy because I realized I was angry at the injustice of a painful existence, in what I was becoming to understand was a blameless world. We were weak, fleshy, we bruised and cut ourselves, we became sick, we starved, we hurt each other, and watching someone suffer was a heartache that was unbearable.

I originally considered myself as some kind of savior, giving the world something with the power to change some of the things that caused grief in life. People would never get sick, they could take a plant that would heal them, and would live as long as they liked for as long as they took the plant. They could always be healthy and never have to be afraid of pain or death. It was an answer.

I could only just start to see how terrible it really was. Nothing stopped the obscene. I had been offered another chance and this time it would be a chance to damn the world on real and authentic grounds. Not reasons covered with a thin veneer of altruism, but reasons of abuse, spite, and anger and I was choosing them willingly. I tried being the savior, then the victimized, I imagined myself a martyr, and now, I was nothing. I had no vindication or defense. I did something so impossibly and heartbreakingly wrong, and no one would stop it, because they wanted the plant for the same reasons I had shared it to begin with. It wouldn't matter that some might not take it, what mattered is that some would.

I look back at Maria as she stares out into the countryside, lost in her own thoughts.

"Their mothers have been good to them, and they have been good to their mothers. They will like it. It will help them eat. They will like them. They will help them," she says. "It will be good for us from now." She looks at the basket and clenches her teeth. "Michael, I am not happy from you, but you are okay, they will be happy and have their home."

I would be demanding payment for my suffering, and I would be demanding it from the very people afflicted with it. Paul knew people would take the plant willingly. He never thought the plant itself was good or bad, only that people would take it anyway, and when they did, they would need to be cared for. "It won't matter."

We would be monsters to the innocent. There was nothing to stop the sheer unthinkable horrors to come. I had been wrestling for days to understand my actions while needing to make decisions, and retrospect is a slingshot.

"Michael, I don't know. Is it..?" Holding her hand out flat in the air and bringing it up and down.

There is going to be an explosion coming in by the fence in front of the fourth loading dock. We need you to leave. There are 23 of them. They're Grippers.

"What?"

Bring another screener in the room, he's picking this up.

"What?"

"I said good or happy bad, Michael?" Maria said again. I looked and the basket was gone. A chime rang on the patio, which meant David wanted to see Maria. I'd only heard it once before. She rose out of her seat and hurried through the door inside.

The space between two moments is endless, as any scientist will explain quickly and to no point. I don't remember what happened next. The door opened and Maria said, "David wants to see you."

Walking inside, David is standing on the stairs. "Michael," he says.

Flames dart across my vision and my mind is hurtled backward and I slam into the ground. I can't breathe.

Sir, we're having a problem. You're going to need to come back out here.

There's a serious problem, Michael is--

Get another screener in here. Put him under, bring it back to the maid.

I don't care.

"Michael, I am not happy from you, but you are okay, they will be happy to work and have their place."

"Alright," I say.

"It is good what you are doing."

"It won't matter," I say.

"You're going to London, I want you to be ready in three hours."

"What's in London?" I ask.

"Matthew Rindale. He's the one who sold Wendy the plant."

"Alright," I say.

"We'll find you some more clothes there," he says, waving away any concerns I might have before dismissing me.

I walked back up to the guest room I'd been staying in since my first night and looked into the mirror behind the dresser. My face was clay, my eyes were sunken. I looked like a criminal inside of a criminal's skin. I ran my fingers through my dark hair. I could not see myself.

I looked down at the bag lying on the dresser, it was warm from the sunlight. The drapes were pulled back and the blinds were open only slightly. The room was slightly chilly after having been outside, but a shaft of light fell from between the blinds on to the satchel I could not live without. I slowly waved my hand through the light and it was just clear space.

"Michael, what are you doing?" Dr. Lockard asks from the doorway looking out the window behind me.

"Nothing," I say.

"Are you okay, Michael?"

My eyes were a tunnel and a kaleidoscope, they slid off of hers and I couldn't make a connection.

"You don't look okay," she says. She was wearing a pink shirt with a collar.

They had given me some of Emanuel's old clothes. They didn't fit well, but I had stopped caring about the fate of anything at all. "I'm okay," I said.

"You don't look good," she repeats.

"It's okay, it doesn't matter."

Shrugging, she takes her hand off the door frame and turns to leave.

The space between anything is oblivion.

I picked up my bag and went out into the woods where I would usually dose. I had never seen anyone out there. David never came around. Emanuel tried talking to me, at times, as did Wendy, when she came by, but I had stopped responding. There was no pretense. Dr. Lockard checked on me occasionally. I grew listless until I finally decided there was nothing I would be able to do otherwise. I was trying to prove to myself that I had some sense of morality or honor. I realized there wasn't any in anyone, just countless dreams and nightmares that may or may not be.

David told me to bring the satchel with me on our way to London. I forgot to ask him about the airport and whether there would be a problem. I don't remember why I had forgotten.

I sat in the woods, finding only peace in solitude. I only saw fear in my mind now when on Bloodleaf.

Behind me, I noticed a man and woman approaching and could faintly hear them talking.

They're breaking in, Jon. Shut it down. Jola, Kori, we stay here, hold him in and hold him down. We've got to do something. Bring him to the plane. I don't care, just do it.

I don't understand what is happening to me.

He's tucked, Jola.

I looked out through the opening to the cockpit and saw David sitting quietly, it looked like he was sleeping.

"Why did you sell the plant, Michael?" Dr. Lockard asked.

"We didn't sell it."

"How did you find it?" She was sitting nearby, the plane was small, designed for comfort. It was quiet.

"I worked on one of the travel ships to Horizon. The crew is allowed to stay until they're needed on a ship back. I liked Horizon a lot, it's different from Earth. You don't feel the same way when you're there. I applied for a position as crew on one of the ships and they had taken me. I didn't have many people in my life. I was interested and eager. I was polite and I kept to myself. I was innocent and I guess that's why people will choose someone. I was just happy to be a part of something that big and I wasn't allowed to talk about it very much to anyone back home. I kept to myself, anyway, most of the time. I had just wanted to get out."

"What is Horizon like?" she asked.

"When you go through the gateway to Horizon the sand is red and flat. You can't see well off into the distance, it fades and blurs and it hurts your eyes. You have to keep the ground in mind. You eventually settle out and adjust. It affects your sense of balance. It's difficult to explain, you're given steps to adjust."

I thought about it a bit more, sorting through ways to explain the differences in a way she'd understand. "We were warned not to let someone stare out into the distance too long. That's how we called it in New Civ. It wasn't mentioned much, it was just 'out there'. If you did though, you would start to have problems. We had to stay by passengers a lot until they adjusted. You really have to carefully take everything in for a while. You're supposed to keep an eye on others and look out for anyone who was staring out for too long. You could tell if someone had been doing it, though."

I looked over at Dr. Lockard. She was lost in thought and then started blinking quickly.

"It's hard to imagine," she said.

"It's different for everyone. There's a lot of focus on

everything, but it's fun. You stay inside a lot, but there's a good amount to do. There's a feeling there that you can't explain. It was good to come home though. You feel the weight of everything here. It's comfortable, but you understand once you return that we're supposed to leave."

"I would ask people who stayed and worked in New Civ as many questions as I could. It wasn't unusual at all. There were speeches you could go to, various events. No one was afraid of anything, it was too massive and open. We were told in one of the lectures that it was endless, but I don't understand how. They said it was larger than anything conceivable."

"What do you mean 'we're supposed to leave'?" she said.

"That's not something easy to explain. You start to understand that we're not supposed to stay here on Earth."

"Why?"

"Because of all the weight. I don't understand how to explain it. We're not supposed to stay here, we come from here."

She seemed offended. "What's wrong with Earth?" she asked.

"Nothing," I said.

"Tell me about Horizon."

"There's a stone, it's like a crystal, hanging off in the sky above New Civ. It's filled with a light that flows like liquid and it lights up the whole area. For a while, it will stay at its brightest and then it will slowly dwindle down until it's dark for about half a day or so, by Earth's standards. It's different, so you would get used to when different groups did things. When it was dark, though, an observation tower would study the area. When I started with the crew, they had already finished building it.

"It's funny, a lot of passengers thought it was fun to try and stay awake for the whole time it was bright, but you can't. They try, but no one can really do it. It's a few days long. Most of the people who stay there follow their own routine, but a lot of people who stay will sleep during the night out of habit. You can see other lights farther off when it's night, if you can bear to look. We mostly stayed inside."

"It sounds very beautiful, Michael," she said.

"It is. The crystals are different sizes. They don't have the same kind of light in all of them and they're everywhere."

"Where do you think they come from?"

"Why are you asking?" I demand, and more forcefully than I intended.

"I mean, what causes them to be there? Do you think there are other people out there, Michael?" she says.

I was bathing in witch hazel and my body felt cold. Something left me and evaporated from my breath. All that remained was a spectre stretched out over hundreds of years. I fell back into the coldest lake imaginable.

"Michael, what is going to happen?" she said.

I said something, but couldn't hear myself. I turned to look at her and my eyes were misty.

On the plantation, I would go to the woods nearby to dose so I wouldn't see the thoughts of the few people who stayed in the mansion, mainly from fear. It was during this time I learned that David and Dr. Lockard were father and daughter. They had come close enough or I had not gone out far enough during this revelation.

David rarely stayed very long and he refused to come near me. As they unknowingly came close to where I was, I saw that David held absolutely no concern or care for my life in any way, shape or form. He admired only the fact that I had something that he wanted, and he would take it and be done. I was nothing to him, whatever I said or did would not matter. He viewed me as a coward, I viewed myself as a coward, and I had what he wanted and was pitying myself.

I stayed away from everyone. I could not even bring myself to do or think about my actions or the consequences. Any action I took would simply slip my own bearings into a sheer and absolute meaninglessness, a place of no substance, no right or wrong, and no real connection to anything at all. He felt my attempts at salvaging any self-worth were a waste of time, proving I had no worth with each passing day. I was nothing to him.

His daughter's name was Jen and she became more personal with me over time.

David told her to do whatever she wished in life and he would help her. She earned her degree as Jennifer Lockard. She spent most of her time alone in her youth.

David took care of the few people he did know, if not respect, the only way he knew how. He gave people what they wanted by taking it from someone who had it or by giving them something in return. It did not matter to him. He usually asked Jen to join him in his work and help him with what he did.

She ended up further retreating into her own mind behind a complicated web of strained relationships built upon deception. She quickly realized she was becoming further isolated from herself and anyone else who could have mattered to her. I did not want to know any of this. I did not want to know anything at all.

She asked me something again and I replied, but couldn't hear it. I rubbed my eyes and she paled and sighed as if something deep was becoming unsettled and falling into place.

"Michael, you're doing this wrong," she said. "You're making everyone lose something, you're making everyone pay."

"There's no other way to cross." I said, looking out through a window on the side of the plane, down at the silver and tarnished ocean, the dissolved metal which had never stopped existing, filled with lightning and life, but I would never be there, in that space, at that moment. I was only allowed to see it.

"When I was a girl, I thought that maybe this place was something special. Maybe it was some place far greater than we could ever really imagine. Somewhere, in some way, things could work out alright." Letting out a small laugh and wiping her eye with a monogrammed handkerchief, she says, "I don't believe there is a God anymore," and sighs. "Isn't that terrible?" she asks, raising the handkerchief to her face once more. "I don't understand how this place can be special at all. It can't be."

"It can be," I assure her.

"Why are you doing this, Michael?"

"I thought I was doing something right. I'm not."

"Is that why? You wanted to do what was right?"

"No," I said.

"It doesn't make any sense."

"I know."

"Why don't you feel anything about it, Michael?"

I tried to share something with her that I was trying to understand myself. "It's the distance people need to make and what they do or don't want to share, and why it's so important that they do or don't share it, or can, or will, or have it heard and be heard. I wanted to do something right, and it wasn't, and it's beyond anything that anyone can do anymore, and that's why it hurts."

She bit her lip. "When does it stop?"

"I don't know," I said.

"I wanted to make the world a better place," she says, looking haunted.

"I did, too."

"If people won't die, or can live a very long time, then it doesn't have to be bad and things can be made better. Why can't you believe that?"

Jola, bring him out. He's going down, he's not responding. He hears us, but he's not responding.

I don't care.

Sen Jola, I wish we had not made this agreement. He was fine the way he was.

I don't understand why we cannot have him conscious and aware of what's happening around him. That's all, Kori. You know what I'm saying. It's important that we do this and prove we can do it.

You and every one of... you who started this, Jola! Not 'we'. I did not want to hear any of this. We did not need to know this. If he dies then we all die, do you understand?

You know what I said. He might understand what's happening. I can't believe tha--

You're putting memories into his head! You're changing his memories and it's not right! You don't even know how much of this is madness, Jola!

What about a history that you didn't even know about, Kori? I'm trying to bring him through to some kind of sanity! He has to make it through all of this, intact and somewhat whole, or he's gone! You didn't even know--

I'm wracked with pain and I start shaking. Jen screams and David yells from the front of the plane. The cabin breaks apart and I'm falling into nothing and my throat is hoarse. Something is forcibly shoved into my mouth and I bite down on it trying to scream.

I remember someone once told me a poem, they painted an image, they had given me something in a way that can't be given. They said something would happen at a different time and this was how I believed everything. I could paint it, or sing it, or show it and it is only oak trees in a meadow, and they are black ink that soaks into a dark blue sky and holds up the ground from falling and this where you can find anything you set your mind to, and put it back up as it flows. When I do this, I rest and I fear.

Move back, move back! Let it pass. Just let him calm down.

It stays.

"Michael. Michael, can you hear us?"

It stays, sometimes.

"It won't last. It can't, and you know it," Michael says.

Another voice speaks up. "What do we do, Michael?"

"It was too late once it started. You have to go to Horizon," Michael says.

"What is that, Michael?"

"Go to the gateway. Get everyone to the gateway."

"What gateway?" Jola asks.

"The one to Horizon," Michael says.

"There is no gateway, Michael. What is Horizon? We know you've seen it, but there isn't one. Earth isn't like what you're... It's not like that. Are you talking about Avena? There's no other dimension. We don't know what's wrong with you. We don't know what happened to you," Jola says.

Michael opens his eyes briefly, then closes them and lies still.

The hum in the room flickers. Kori pulls a small plastic card from the pocket of his brown and creased linen pants and presses his thumb to a corner and holds it there. Soon, a door opens nearby and he turns and leaves. Jola looks after him to stop him and is furious.

Walking down the hallway, Kori kept his mind on whatever floated through it, no real care or worry. Always looking forward to the future, hopeful and optimistic. Briefly, he considers stopping in the cafeteria but rejects the idea, because Chalea would be there. She would always let everyone know that she would gaze him and no one would stop her, because Kori didn't like to be gazed, and it showed.

Pulling the card from his pocket again, he pressed his thumb to it. Looking around, several armed security greedily chewed their gazelace, saliva dripping down their chins and the corners of their mouths, they were stupid and fierce, and stood much taller than anyone else. They filled the short and narrow hallway with their body heat. Grotesquely fat arms and misshapen bodies, ugly in anyone's eyes who did not love people made this way, ugly to those who were not allowed to have arms so large, or strong, or were so vicious and cruel. One of them watched Kori, it's eyebrows cruel and dark, it's face contorted and eyes small, gazing Kori, sucking saliva back into his mouth and chuckling.

The door opened and Kori stepped through, placing the card back into his pocket as he went. He stepped onto the lifter, just a slow and easy glide up a few stories higher. He knew where he was going. He thought of the other guard, how it stood slack and dull, how large the guards were and became a little frightened when he thought of how painful it would be to do something they wouldn't like. The lifter stopped and the door in front of him slid open. Walking forward, he looked for the third door on the left, or was it the second door, and he realized it was the third after all. Pressing two of the three buttons on the panel, then pressing one twice, it opened.

The room was dark, in the middle was a glowing perimeter of bright flickering lines, fanning outwards and downwards as they opened for him. He was one of the very few to ever see it.

Walking up, he stepped onto the platform. It folded up around him, and in the flash of an eye, he was gone.

Someone in the cafeteria laughed, and Chalea waited, smiling and looking around. She thought Kori was so handsome and quiet. He looked older and was mysterious. He always minded being gazed. She never noticed him with gazelace and she wanted to take it with him.

Jola looked at the clock. "Shit." Wiping his forehead, he looks around at his equipment. The three screeners were silent. They had no choice, with no minds to speak of and their vocal folds removed. They had probably broken serious laws, but Jola knew the laws enforced were arbitrary at times.

Screeners were always needed, but everyone was always kept unaware of how many there were at any given time. He was medical and never bothered to count. Counting was simple and he had no need. "Jon, we are severely running out of time. Something's wrong with Michael and if Kori tells anyone about what we're doing, I have no idea what is going to happen. We need to keep Michael alive," Sen Jola says.

"Is... is what..?" Jon replies.

"Don't ask me anything, you didn't see anything, you don't know anything, you are not to leave this room until this is finished, do you understand, Jon? You are not to take gaze again until after we're finished, do you understand?"

"Yes, Sen Jola," Jon says.

Shaking, he drops a metal pan on the ground filled with gazelace.

Looking back from the resuscitation console to the ground, Sen Jola reaches out. "Give me that, Jon! Now!" he says, holding out his hand.

Stammering, Jon's hands begin to shake. Looking down at the mess on the floor, he is unable to move. Snatching the pan from Jon, Jola bends down, angrily picking up the ropes of gazelace and throwing them back into the pan.

"You are not to touch these, you got it?" Jola says.

"But... but I'd have to..." Jon begins saying.

"Be quiet!" he shouts and Jon quiets down. Pressing a spot on his cheekbone in front of his right ear, there's a muddled click heard under the skin.

"Sen Stegan, are you there?" Jola asks. He waits and places the pan with the gazelace on a table nearby. "I need you to send another medical student. No, I don't care which one. Pick one. I need one as soon as possible. Tell him he needs a Vac, too.

There's been an accident. One of the Casted students was found locked in the resuscitation room. No, I don't know which one, he didn't have an ID on him. I know. I know. Oh yes, that's right. Jon. If it was Jon, I'm going to feel miserable, he was supposed to help me on a project. Yes. Yes, I understand. Tell them as soon as possible. Yes, yes, I know. I need the Vac as soon as possible. Yeah. Thanks. For awhile. I know. Thank you. You too."

Turning around Jola sees Jon is still and lying on the ground.

Pulling up the front of Jon's shirt, he looks for the death patch that would be stuck to his abdomen.

Jola clicks near his ear again. "Stegal? Tell him to hurry, it's a mess." Reaching down, he absently takes a rope of gazelace and begins chewing it lightly. Looking back at the console he hits a button which stimulates Michael's hypothalamus with a clearing agent and starts entering terse commands into the simulator.

"It's down at the end, Michael. We need to understand who else is taking the plant."

Suddenly, I feel comfortable and warm.

"I don't know, she's heading towards the GSS embassy. Don't ask me that." David is casually walking along the crowded sidewalk with his hands in his pockets. I try and adopt his posture while people brush past us completely unaware of who we are.

"It's up here," he says, pointing at one of the buildings. David turns to look at me and takes something out of his pocket. It's four small and flat metal rings encircling each other with a flat disc in the middle and he hands it to me. There's some kind of gear mechanism inside of it. It has a good heft and weight. I push and pull at the rings, they turn slowly, with good resistance.

"What is this thing, David?"

"Monbloc, Matthew's clothing shop."

"No, I mean, what is this?" I ask, holding up the rings.

"Come on, Michael," he turns briefly to look at me when I don't move, "Use that if you get stressed again. Dr. Lockard is worried you're developing some mental crises."

I place the device into my pocket and look through one of the windows. The place is moderately crowded with people looking through the racks of clothes. It's night time and people are walking past us on the street. The general hum is occasionally pierced with people calling to each other. The street ends at an intersection and across the way is a grassy area, a park with benches, and trees leave shadows.

I look back through the window. "You're going to go in there?"

"We need to talk to him alone," David says. "We need to find out where everyone is that is taking the plant."

"Alright," I say. "I haven't seen any... I haven't seen anyone I know in a long time." I say, pulling my jacket tighter, hiding.

Looking down, then looking back at me, David says, "He doesn't know you're coming. Stay out here. I'll come back for you."

Looking around at the street full of strangers, I shake my head, "No, I'll come with you."

"Do you recognize anybody in there?"

I look through the window again. "No."

"Alright. Find some clothes that fit you while I talk to him."

Instead of following, I turn and look down into the park. An oblong shape catches my attention, it rests on a pedestal and is too dimly lit to make out any details.

"Michael?" David's voice snaps me back from the dark shape in the park.

"I'm trying to remember something that I don't know that... I did."

"What?" David asks.

I turn and look back at David.

Suddenly, I'm compelled to ask, "Is any of this real, David?"

It's nighttime. The building is old. People are walking by, loose dirty papers blow through the street and are stepped on. I'm not looking at anyone. No one cares. I'm looking at the scenery, I'm a bystander, I'm avoided.

"I know I am," David says.

CHAPTER 7

Walking into the shop together, David makes his way over towards a girl standing behind a counter. She doesn't recognize him and his posture remains easy and casual. He affects a simple and breezy attitude and she buys it. I notice from the corner of my eye that she smiles.

I walk over to a row of hanging shirts and idly flip through them while a couple standing next to me are talking. The man is explaining he is not interested in wearing clothes like the ones she pulled out for him.

"Come on, Charles, you need something really classy, really distinguished, you know?" she says, and she gives him a nudge. Her eyes are bright and she grins as she turns back to the clothing rack.

He grumbles and whispers something in her ear.

"No, I'm serious," she says, slapping him on the chest. "Come on, quit it. Look, look at this guy here." She stumbles over the word.

"Hey, you," she says to me, still grinning and looking me in the eye. "Hey, you, can I call you that? You? Can I call you, you? You are you, aren't you?"

"Don't listen to her, she's cracked," the man tells me in a confidential tone.

"Shut up, Charles. I'm going to ask him a question."

"Don't answer, she's cracked. She's cracked." He's tall. His skin is tan and his hair is black.

"Tommy! Tommy, come here!"

I'm standing completely still and my hand is shaking.

"Tommy!"

"Who?" the man says. "Him? You mean me?"

I'm trying to pull myself together and the man suddenly looks at me and says, "Hey, are you alright?"

I'm standing still with my hand in the air and it's shaking badly. I'm flooded with memories back to the time after I was arrested. I suddenly realize how easily I could be locked up or tortured again with no way to escape, how easily my words were turned and twisted and used against me.

A hand hits my back and I see Matthew Rindale. He was similar to how I remembered him, and he still had the same mustache that made him look like a cartoon character. He had the subtle signs of good health and it had been a while since I had seen this, I didn't recognize them right away. He just had the air of someone you wanted to be jealous of and get to know without knowing why.

"Tommy! It's so good to see you!" He hugs me tightly and whispers in my ear, "You need to tell them to go away, but don't make a scene. Just be nice," he says.

"I'm sorry, it was very nice running into you," I say to the couple.

Matthew whispers in my ear again, "Say something to the gentleman, he's tense." Matthew still has his arm draped over my shoulder, "We're all friends here," he reminds me.

"Don't get into any trouble," I say. The man, Charles, blushes.

"Tommy, come on, come on. I've got the hat you ordered, come on, come this way," he says, pulling me away from the couple.

"You are you," I hear behind me. "You are really something else, Melly."

Matthew is gripping my arm painfully.

"Come on, Tommy," he says.

We walk through a door in the back of the shop and Matthew turns to me. "What are you doing, Michael?" he whispers fiercely.

"What do you mean?"

"I thought you were dead! I thought you were on your way to fucking outer space where none of this is happening!" It's hard for him to keep his voice low. He's angry. David is nowhere around.

"I was. The boat wrecked on the way there. Why are you angry? Do you know what they did to me?"

"Michael, do you watch the news?" He's pissed.

"No?"

"China, the United States, Germany, France... a few others... they just gave GSS sanctions to act! They did it tonight!" He's counting off the countries on his fingers.

"Any country that allows it! Everyone's falling in line! They're washing their hands of the whole thing! All they have to do is take care of themselves and play along, now. No nasty diplomatic or domestic issues. It's everywhere! How come you haven't heard?"

"I don't understand what you mean," I say.

"It means Global Security and Safety is allowed to make and enforce laws for anyone, no matter where they live. It's a sweep! There's nowhere to run! They aren't even a fucking *nation*, man. They work in a country, they're not a part of one! Who defers to who? Who has control now? Oh, it's all well and good, people take care of themselves, that's what I always say. Oh, it's such a sweet deal, no more politicians wasting time worrying about everyone else. Everyone's all protected from each other, now no one has to worry about anything anyone else is doing because... oh god, it's a fucking scam, we're all fucked! Get in here! Come on!"

Still muttering to himself, we enter a room with a table and a dim light. David is sitting down and doesn't look up at me. Matthew pulls out a chair and says, "Sit down," and he slaps his hand down on the table.

"Look, I don't know what's happened to you, Michael, but you need to understand something. These people have no natural allegiance," he turns to David. "Am I offending any political sensibilities you might have, Davey?"

David is still looking down in his hands and typing with his thumbs. "You're not offending me, Jacko,"

"I didn't think so," he looks off and then turns to me. "They have no natural allegiance, Mike. Global? Allegiance? It's pure crap, do you understand? A man lives in a country and he defends it. You stand for your territory, you protect your home. It's natural. That's what a country is, that's how it's worked out. You can't protect it all from its very self, and you sure can't protect something if you're not even a part of it. You can't have no allegiance to anything and just run everything."

"Amen, brother," David says without looking up.

"You can't have an allegiance to a place that we are all a part of and that we are all also set against each other, too. Think about it. Everyone fucking hates everyone. No one ever agrees on anything. You can't say you're protecting the whole world and not have a stake in it. Who are you protecting the world from? Itself? It's bullshit."

"We don't all work together, that's the point. I can barely keep myself from packing up and leaving my old lady, but I try not to, because every day I remind myself I love her and she is the most wonderful woman I have ever met and I wouldn't be anywhere without her and she'll kill me, anyway. If someone broke into our house and held a gun to my head and said I had to get along with her, I'd say let me go get the shower curtain, lay it down on the carpet, real careful and nice, so the carpet won't get stained and make her mad before she gets back, okay?"

"You can't have something that protects the interest and safety of 'all the citizens of this one place in which we all here and a part of' and not also be a part of it and protect itself from *itself*. Oh, GSS will protect us, it's friends, from our enemies, which is us, our... enemies. It doesn't make a lick of sense. That's what your own country is supposed to do."

"It doesn't stand up. It's one of those... it's one of those *contradictoral...*" he stops and takes a breath, "It's a complete scam. It can't work. It's fucked, buddy. Who is this guy anyway, Michael?" he says, waving his hand at David.

I look back at Matthew. "David Johnson. I thought you knew him?"

"Yeah. Yeah, I know *of* him. I know Wendy, Michael. I just started talking with David."

"Wendy's my wife, Matt." David says.

"I know. Fuck me, I'm sorry," he says, looking contrite for a moment.

David sniffs and finishes typing.

Matthew sighs and finally sits down in a chair. Wiping his hand across his face, he gives me a hard stare. "Michael, what happened to you? I thought you were dead. Paul's dead, Mike. Paul died."

"I know," I said.

His chest caves in and he looks off. "He's dead," he says again softly.

"What happened?" I'm unable to think or feel anything.

"He stopped showing up. He disappeared. His apartment was raided a few months ago, there was a big do about it."

"How did they...?"

"You can't murder someone that way. I don't know if he had any 'leaf on him, but I'm going to assume that it's safe to say that he didn't."

I can't think of anything.

"I'm sorry, man," Matthew says.

"When was the last time you talked to him? Did he say anything?" I ask.

"He did. He told me to tell you something if I ever saw you again." He turns towards David and looks at me.

"What did he say?" I ask, my body starts shaking even before hearing the answer.

"He said it only works with you," Matthew says. "He said you're the only one who can grow the plant."

"You tried to grow one here?"

"Paul did. He tried. He said it has something to do with the first one you grew. He tried to clip one of them and grow it, but it didn't work. You've got to be there, that's what he said."

"How many do you have, Matthew?" David asks.

"Three. They're going on two feet, one of them's near three," he says.

"Are they here?" David asks.

"Yeah, we keep them hidden. I'm not showing you where they are. It was bad enough I gave Wendy one to open this place," he pauses. "Everyone's here in London now."

"Is there anyone new involved?" David asks and rises out of his seat.

Matthew shifts a bit and gives David an uneasy look.

"We're not really... Let's just say this GSS shit's got us too afraid to spit toothpaste when we're brushing our teeth."

David slaps him on the back, "Well you look good, Matthew, really healthy," and he places an emphasis on this last part. "It was a good idea to get this close to the embassy with everything going on,"

"Yeah, thank Paul, he's the one who came up with the idea," Matthew says. He looks up and makes a cross over his chest and face. "God rest his soul."

"Alright, Michael, come on. We're going to stay the night and head back in the morning. Keep in touch, Matthew," David says.

"Are you really going to grow the plant, Michael?" Matthew turns to ask me.

I look back at David. He nods.

"Yeah, I think so. It'll take a while," I say. I stand up and grab my satchel, wrapping the strap securely around my shoulder. As David and I are walking to the door, Matthew places his hand on my arm and grasps it firmly. "Remember, Michael. GSS is a world power with no affiliation to anything in the world. There's no natural allegiance to anything on it."

"Think about that," he says, squeezing my shoulder.

Looking down the hallway and then back at me, David asks, "You coming?"

"Yeah," I respond, feeling empty from the exchange.

"Alright," he says. The hallway is dark, the angles of his face are sharp and I see a vein that trails and wanders over his temple. He's older, but his hair is prematurely white. It's thin and short. His eyes are blue, his nose is long and it has a bump where it angles downward. His lips are thin, and his cheeks are hollow, but he's strong. He's not a short man, but he gives that impression. He looks like he's made of wood, but it doesn't take long to see that he has iron in him, somewhere. He is a man who could be anything to anyone.

I turn to say goodbye to Matthew, but he's sitting at the table and wiping his mustache and looking off in the distance thinking to himself. I imagine at any other time he would have had an ashtray, dead cigarette butts in it filled to the top, and one already lit that he would be reaching for. Instead, he was rubbing his arms, nervously. He wasn't wearing an apron, but that was the feeling he gave. His forearms were large and he was overweight, but he was gentle with his hands, they were soft. He had the demeanor of a man who stressed and worried and just wanted to be a chef somewhere, rather than live the life he was given.

CHAPTER 8

"He's "He's lying about sharing the plant," David remarks. We were stopping for fuel before beginning our trek across the ocean. Jen was quiet, lost in her own thoughts. She looked worried and haunted, but when I would look again, she would be smiling and seem innocent. I didn't understand this and started worrying for my own sanity, which was suspect as it was.

"Why do you say that?" Jen asks him.

"He's not stupid, but he cares too much about people. He can't keep them from talking, he can't keep husbands from telling wives, brothers telling sisters. He's worried because the people who are taking it have families."

"So what if they take it?" she asks him.

"He doesn't have enough and he knows it."

"What are you planning, David?" I ask.

"First, we're going to get back and wait for Wendy. Several people will be coming through over the next few months."

I gripped my satchel tightly. I would need to dose again soon.

Jen turns to me and says "What happened when you found the plant, Michael?"

Shit.

Jen turns to me and says "What happened when you found the plant, Michael?"

Shit. Shit. What is that sound? What the hell are you doing?

Look, I'm trying to sit here, I don't know what else you want me to do!

It's very simple! Do you want to live? Do you even know what that means? I need you to feed these screeners and don't touch anything, or make a bunch of noise, or tap your feet, or drum your fingers, or anything. I don't have the time right now, this is extremely important!

Who is that?

He's one of our mental patients, we're trying to recover his sanity. Please don't touch anything, and don't ask questions, this is an extremely delicate procedure.

Why does he look so... old?

Look, if you want something to do, why don't you plug in and leave me alone?

I can't.

Why?

I'm barred.

What, from all of it?

No, just the good places.

How can you be a medical student and also be barred from any V-group?

I don't know, I can't remember.

How can you...? What? They tell you! They keep a file! Here, hold on. Let me find it. Here, take this passkey, look up a Vindy and give them a number from this passkey and they'll run it and say the Sen needs you wiped clean, okay?

Alright! You got a place to plug in?

Yeah, there's an area by the table over there. Just sit down and shut up.

Somehow, I'm flying through rain.

"... Paul and I called this girl we knew and her boyfriend. We were flipping out. We talked about it the whole night. We slept and the next night we called them. Paul was amazed by what the plant did. I'd gotten back from Horizon and put the plant on a windowsill. A few weeks later I decided to make tea with it, I didn't understand what I was doing. There were a lot of things going on at the time. My desk was in front of a window. I lived on the fourth floor of a large apartment building with Paul. I was given a few weeks off when I got back from Horizon with the plant. I just got this idea to make tea from it. I broke off some of the leaves, boiled some water. I was sitting in one of the chairs in the apartment, thinking about it. I grabbed a mug, I placed some of the leaf in the water, steeped it and I drank it."

I stopped, remembering the moment it happened. "The water was hot and it scalded my tongue. Then that just went away. Then all of a sudden everything changed."

"When Paul got home, I told him about what happened. I had already told him about the plant being from Horizon. He couldn't believe what I told him. When he came back that night, I made the tea again."

I paused and tried to remember, sweeping the cobwebs off old and dusty memories I could not escape. Clamps and vices that circled my mind, over and over, trying to find redemption inside and unable.

"We talked through most of the night. We really thought it could change everything. It was powerful. We asked one of our friends to come over and he brought his girlfriend and we shared it with them." Gritting my teeth, I continued with my story. "Paul and I had this energy for a while. We were really excited. We were possessed by something we didn't understand and it was huge. I would draw and write all of these different things that didn't make any sense, but we knew it was about what would happen. We couldn't even imagine it."

"About two days later, we were sitting in the living room of our apartment and Rick and his girlfriend were banging on the door. When they came in, they didn't look good at all and they said it was the plant and we knew right away that it was. Rick went to the kitchen and kind of fell on the counter and Beth was crying. Paul and I were terrified and we didn't know what to do and we started yelling."

"Rick started falling apart, right there in the kitchen. Blood was running out of his nose and mouth. It was terrible. Beth was sitting down next to him and Paul went and got one of the leaves from the plant because we knew it healed you and it was the only thing we could do. Even if it was making them sick, it would at least heal them. Rick was gone. Paul gave Beth the plant and like that, she just grew. I mean, she just came back, it was over. It's fast. There was nothing wrong with her and her hand and leg were soaked in blood. Paul and I were sick and he took a blanket and some towels out of a closet and laid them on the kitchen floor and I tried to help her up. I didn't even understand what he was doing. He didn't understand what he was doing. I think we were both just apologizing, we were crying and all we could say was that we were sorry over and over again. There was nothing. The towels and blankets started staining black."

"She looked at us and grabbed some of the dishes off the counter and slammed them to the floor. She was looking for a way to kill us. She wanted to, we wouldn't have stopped her. She tried to slam the door closed as she left. We never saw her again. Nobody came after us. No one asked us anything."

The plane was quiet the rest of the way back. I slept and my dreams were feverish about another life.

David placed a hand on my shoulder. "Wake up, we have a problem."

I opened my eyes and my face was tight. David was breathing heavier, his tongue played across his teeth, his face had more color, his pupils were dilated as he looked at me.

"What's wrong?" I asked, without thinking.

"Grab your bag. Marcus took Wendy's plant."

"What?" I said, trying to sit up, to wake up and get alert. I couldn't. My mind was in a fog and I needed to dose soon.

"Marcus has the plant. No one has found him. We have about twenty minutes before we get back. I've got a vehicle ready, so let's go, we need to get back as soon as we can."

He's talking to me as we're leaving the plane. A large man with a rifle slung over his shoulder, wearing sunglasses, although night was coming, stood next to the vehicle.

"Where's Jen?" I asked.

"She's taking care of something else. Come on," he says, pulling at me to move faster.

I hop into the backseat and the armed man sits next to me, placing the rifle gently between his knees, poised. He takes off his sunglasses.

"It's going to get dark quickly," David says from the front passenger seat. I couldn't see who was driving the vehicle as it started to pick up speed. It was cooling down, but it still felt as if we were in an oven after being in the airplane.

"How do you know Marcus took it? Did he steal the whole plant, or do you mean he ate it?"

He quieted down for a moment and looked around.

"Wendy left the plant in her room and Marcus broke in and grabbed it."

"How do you know? Has he taken it?"

"Judging by what our guys are saying, he has eaten it."

"Where is he now? Is he in a car? He could be anywhere!"

"All of the vehicles are tracked. He's stupid, but he knows that much. I don't know what he's going to do. I want you to dose when we get there and see if you can find him."

"Alright," I say.

The driver clicks on the headlights.

"Now, Michael, I want to ask you a question."

The man next to me grips the gun.

"How serious are you about growing this plant?" David asks.

"I don't think I have a choice, David," I say.

The vehicle picks up its speed.

We hit a few ruts in the ground and the man next to me laughs.

"Carlos," David says.

"Y'ah," the man next to me yells.

"Hit him, but don't kill him," he says, referring to Marcus.

"How do you mean?" Carlos asks.

"That plant he's got, when he eats it, he's not going to be bleeding anymore, or be missing that hand you shot off," David says.

"Like a vampire?"

"No, he can die, that's why I want you to be careful, but let him know what he's getting for turning on us," David says.

Carlos swallows and grips his rifle tighter. We hit another dip in the path and I grab a bar on the side of the vehicle. Carlos suddenly grins. "You mean, he wasn't supposed to do what he did?"

"No, sir, he definitely did not do what he was supposed to do. I want you to help him understand how painful this is going to be for him," David says.

Carlos laughs again and looks at me.

"What about this dude?" he says. "What's he doing?"

"He's a different type of security, he's going to help us, too."

Carlos eyes me. "He taking orders from me?"

"No, Carlos."

"Damn." He pulls a brown handkerchief from a green and sweat-stained front pocket. "Am I taking orders from him?"

"Who do you take orders from, Carlos?" David asks.

Carlos quiets down. "Right, right."

"I don't want you to get all teary about your friend either, Carlos," David says. The vehicle accelerates again.

"What?" Carlos asks.

"It's Marcus. I want you to hurt him badly. He's fucking you, too. Right now."

"Marcus? He's stupid, I don't think he even knows how he could fuck up. He's so stupid he couldn't fuck up if he tried," Carlos says. He's sitting up straighter.

"Well, he did," David says, "Don't say goodbye, I want him alive, but if he escapes, we are all dead."

"Oh, fuck man," Carlos says. "Don't say that."

"Carlos, we are all dead, every single one of us and everyone we know will die or be sent to prison or worse, so I want you to do to him what he is trying to do not only to you but to all of us. Every single one of us."

"Fuck, man," Carlos says. "You make it sound like he's gonna blow up the world or something."

"Not if he doesn't have a leg to stand on," David replies.

Carlos looks down and then says, "A pot to piss in?"

"That's right, Carlos."

Carlos wipes his face with his hand then looks over at me and hits me on the shoulder. "Hey, what do you call a man with no arms and no legs at your door?"

"What?" I'm unable to understand what he is asking me.

"Matt," he grins.

"I don't get it," I say.

"What do you call a man with no arms or legs swimming in the ocean?"

"What are you talking about?"

"Bob," he says. He hits me again. "You get it?"

Carlos yells up to the front seat. "Hey, this guy is a fucking idiot, you said he's security?" He turns to me again and says "What do you call a guy after you cut off his hands and his tongue and you invite him over for dinner?"

"Shush, Carlos," David says.

He grins widely. "Slim," he says. He looks around uncomfortably. "Man, you really don't have a sense of humor at all," Gripping his rifle tighter, he sits back uneasy.

I tell him a joke I had learned in New Civ. "This guy walks into a butcher's shop and asks for some meat that's from the very top shelf," Carlos looks at me expectantly. "The butcher turns to him and says 'No, I can't give you those,' and so the guy asks him 'Why not?'"

I look over at Carlos. "The butcher says 'Those steaks are too high'."

"This guy is a fucking idiot, David," Carlos says and turns away from me, letting his gun lightly bounce against his knees as we make our way down the dirt road.

He turns back to me. "You're a spook, white boy."

"What?"

"You're a spook. You ain't nothing, you're a ghost."

He reaches over and presses two fingers to my forehead and then firmly pushes my head back.

"A spook," he says. "Anybody there?"

"Shush, Carlos," David says.

Further down the road rain starts to fall. We pick up speed and move through it.

When we arrive at the mansion one of the windows on the second story has been smashed out. It's night time and the rain is falling heavily. Carlos hops out of the vehicle with his rifle and David pulls a small device from his pocket. The voice of another man is coming through it. David signals for Carlos to circle the mansion on the right and a voice from the device says, "He's headed out towards the wooded area to the west."

David looks at me and says, "Alright, I want you to take the plant and see if you can spot him."

I reach into the satchel and take one of the leaves out and begin chewing. I wait a bit, it's cold and quiet aside from the sound of light rainfall. I occasionally hear a shout in the distance and my mind opens. David is standing in front of me and he is focused on the woods behind the mansion and I see Marcus in his thoughts. There are three other men on the other side of the building. Their minds are black, slick, aimed forward. The driver steps up from behind me and I look at him. He's an older man, wearing dark sunglasses, and he is holding a cigarette in his hand, covering it from the rain. "Take this," he says.

I see a skull in his mind, a skeleton wearing his hat, and his clothing, with his dark sunglasses. I take the cigarette. He hands me a lighter.

"Smoke," he says.

I do. He holds both his hands of bone aside my face and I light the cigarette to keep the rain from getting it and I take a drag. I look back over at David and his skin is peeling back, revealing a type of red lace, blue eyes and white hair, his teeth are bone white and he clacks them a few times. My own mind is nothing.

The three men give a shout and head towards the woods.

"Let it go," the driver says.

I throw the cigarette down to the ground and David has returned somewhat to normal, though I see he is concentrating on the device in his hand.

"I want to know if anyone sees anything coming out of the woods," he demands.

I start walking towards the area with David, and the driver stays behind with the car.

We head farther, the house behind us, the other men ahead. I see one of the three men think to fire a shot and another next to him decides to do so and a shot rings out.

David motions for me to duck down and we remain quiet, listening. It is difficult to hear anything with the rainfall.

After a moment the three in the front move deeper into the woods and we hear another shot fire from deeper in and one of the three men drops his gun and falls to his hands and knees.

David moves forward and I follow him. Off farther in the distance, I see Marcus and his mind is blazing yellow and white. He is holding a rifle in one hand, the plant, ripped out of it's pot, was in the other.

"Don't fucking play dumb with me, Michael," he thinks.

David asks if I see him.

"He's out there," I say.

Marcus yells out "I see you!" to the three men over to the right. "Don't think I don't see you!" He laughs. His mind blazes a sharp pink.

Carlos gets down to a knee with his rifle aimed at Marcus. "Marcus, what are you doing, man!" Carlos motions for the man to the right of him to move forward and Marcus begins running towards me and David.

Carlos and the other man fire a shot, one after the other, one and then the next one, and Marcus hits the ground and the two men run towards him.

"Grab the plant," David yells. "You have to get it out of his hands."

I move closer and Marcus enters my mind and looks through my eyes. "I can't fucking believe this shit," Marcus says.

"Why did you take the plant?" I plead.

Carlos and the other man jump on Marcus and kneel on his body. David motions with his hand for me to stay where I am.

"He doesn't have it," Carlos says. The other man finds the plant on the ground nearby. Marcus has been shot in the gut and shoulder, and Carlos continues to restrain him.

"What are you going to do to him, David?" I ask. David looks at the device again and the other man hands him the torn up plant. Marcus and I are close enough to each other to see through each other's eyes and Marcus is bearing an incredible amount of pain and I am taking him inside me. The third man, who had been shot, sits in the dirt patiently and eyes the plant in David's hand.

David places a leaf in Marcus's mouth, and Marcus chews the leaf and his body grows back quickly.

They tie Marcus up and bandage the third man and we head back. The Bloodleaf has worn off for Marcus and I.

"What are you going to do with him?" I ask David again.

He looks off to a building to the right. "We're headed over to a warehouse here, come on, Michael, this is what we do."

We enter the building and there are two large metal crates with bars and a few holes in them. One of the men suddenly hits Marcus in the back of his head with the butt of his rifle and he falls to the ground.

And then the same is done to me.

David stands with his foot on my chest and I am looking up at him with swimming eyes.

"Be a good boy, now," he says.

Marcus and I are each thrown into a separate crate and a leaf is thrown in. One in mine, one in his. We hear the warehouse door clatter loudly as it shuts and it is dark.

Marcus bangs on the side of the metal box he is in. "Fuck!" he shouts.

"Fuck!" he shouts again.

"Fuck, fuck fuck!" he repeats, banging over and over again.

I look down at the leaf lying in front of me.

"Michael?" I hear Marcus say from his box.

"Yeah?" I say.

"How long are we going to be in here?" he asks.

"Until we get out, or they run out of leaves to give us," I tell him.

The banging from his metal box echoes for a long time.

CHAPTER 9

It's been a long time we've been stuck in this box.

"Mickey, what time is it?" Marcus asks me.

Marcus calls me Mickey. Sometimes he calls me Mikey.

"I don't know."

"How long have we been in here?" Marcus asks again.

"I don't know," I say, sighing, he asks me this all the time, and my answer never changes but it hasn't stopped him from asking.

"What do you think they're doing out there?" Marcus asks.

"I don't know," I say.

"What do you know, Mickel?" Sometimes he calls me Michelob.

"I don't know,"

"How come you got to be so crazy? It's only me in here. I'm going to kill the next one that lets me out," he said.

He did. He has. He killed someone. They beat him mercilessly, fed him the plant and beat him again. I cried for a very long time. I cry about it still sometimes, but he doesn't remember why he is scared or sad.

Every few days they drag the crates out into a field and we grow a new plant.

We see the minds of the people around us, but they don't know anything.

I don't know if I'm saying this out loud or not.

"Saying what?" Marcus asks.

"What?" Michael says.

"I said I don't know what's going on," I lean my head back and blazing blue fireworks shoot back and forth across my face, highlighting something I've never seen, and I'm staring down into a long tunnel.

I don't know if I was awake or asleep. Sometimes, you wonder if you tilt your head back far enough if you will ever be able to get back up. I did this so many times that I don't even understand where I am anymore, but a little boy who is me keeps me company. He tied a rope to one of the bars of the crate and has wrapped it around my feet and he swings on it into a rollercoaster.

"Marcus, help me, I'm tied down," I say.

"I'm on the phone, man, hold on," I hear.

"No, really, Marcus. Help me, I'm tied down, I can't move at all." I'm looking at a string tied around my big toe and I can't move at all because I'm tied down.

"Hold on, I've got another call. Yeah, hello? Yeah. No. No, I don't know. Orange. Red. Um, hold on." Marcus covers up the phone.

"Hey, Michael?" Marcus asks.

I wake up. "Yeah?" I say.

"Can you call me back? I'm really busy right now, I'm tied down."

"Okay." I look for a phone, but I can't find one. "I can't find the phone."

"I've got it," Marcus says.

"Okay, good."

"Are you still calling me?" he asks.

"No," I said, "I'm tied down, I can't move."

"Hmm," he thinks awhile. "Can you touch your toes?"

"Hold on." I reach down and touch my toes.

"Yeah, I can touch my toes,"

"How many do you have?" he asks.

"Ten?" The little boy who is me is flying around in an airplane now.

"Okay, can you call me back in a million, billion years?" he says.

"Why?"

"Because I'm lonely."

Marcus is lonely. He is very lonely because he only has himself in the box that he is in and he's not crazy like me. Marcus says I am lucky to have this little boy in the box with me who runs around and plays in a big amusement park. Marcus doesn't have this and now he's very angry but sometimes he listens and he will sing or talk of other things.

"How old am I? I don't remember," Marcus says and he starts banging on the metal box. Loudly. I don't know if I even speak anymore, but I can shout because Marcus will make a loud noise, and I scream, but I cry until I can't care anymore and then I fall again and again and wake up and scream until I wake up again.

"Stop it, Marcus!" I shout.

He keeps banging on the box. "Let me out, let me out, let me out, let me out!" and he screams and cries.

"Marcus, don't do that!"

"Let me out, let me out, let me out!" he says, but now he says other things only he understands.

The little boy who is me runs to the wishing well and will throw a penny in every time Marcus says something like this.

"Did he make a wish, Michael?" Marcus asks.

"Yeah, Marcus,"

"What's it?" Marcus says.

"A marching band," I say and it's true.

"What song are they singing, Michael?" he asks.

I try to sing the music they are playing but the words fall from my lips like heavy strands of drool.

"Michael," Marcus says.

Sometimes we get taken out into the field, and they cut my hand, or my arm, or anything, and they cut him and we look through each other's eyes, but there is nothing to see.

No one understands what we are. It doesn't matter. One out there will think the sun is bright. They love the nighttime and the moon here on Earth. They eat well. They live and love and laugh and fuck each other sometimes because it's all good fun.

There are more and more plants and I can't remember

anything. At times I feel an electric jolt slam through my body. Marcus doesn't feel this, but he screams loudly at times. They beat him a lot because he is violent when they let him out to clean. They've not beaten me and Marcus hates me. He says I am scared. He did, he doesn't say that now, he says he loves me, he says this a lot, but I don't say it back to him because I'm not scared like him. They hit him in the face with a metal bat and knocked out his teeth, but they grew back.

"I love you, Michael," he says.

"I love you, too," I say. I'm afraid of him.

I'm afraid of the little boy who is me, but I'm not afraid, too. I'm not afraid of anything. I was always afraid of everything.

Marcus asks me if I remember when we walked and I said that I did not remember now, because a lot of people have died in the fights that are going on. Marcus tells me about it. He says that a lot of people are getting killed, and he has seen this, but I don't understand this because none of this is real.

This is all fake and made up bullshit.

CHAPTER 10

"Alright, class, does anyone have any questions before I let you out?" Folding her hands together, Mrs. Brendar surveyed the class.

Jake Callen raises his hand without looking up from his notebook. Several people in the classroom look over at Jake, putting their hands to their mouths to yawn, carelessly showing their contempt. Knowing glances among the students shared the thought that this was a complete waste of time and boredom. A few people inched closer in their seats, knowing Jake had a reliable record of giving Mrs. Brendar a hard time in her history class.

Looking around at the rest of the classroom, Mrs. Brendar silently pleaded for someone, anyone, to raise a hand and say "No, we have no questions, Mrs. Brendar, because you always teach us so wonderfully," but no one does. She can ignore Jake a little longer, fantasizing a world without a Jake Callen in it. She savored these bitter moments, as fleetingly as they were. Finally, unclenching her teeth, and without making eye contact, she asks, "Yes, Jake?"

Raising his eyes from his notebook directly at the teacher, he says, "Why are we learning history if we're going to die anyway?"

Packing up his notebook, Robert snaps, "You are always doing this, Jake." In no mood to adhere to the social niceties of not interrupting another student during a discussion, his disgust as plain as the notebook he was holding, he sighs and begins to pack his belongings.

The rest of the class, taking their cues from Robert, begin to chatter lightly about their plans for the upcoming holiday. Kev sits in the back and ducks his head down again and continues drawing on a piece of paper.

"What, I can't ask a question, Rob? At least I ask questions so I can learn instead of just telling everyone what they're doing that I don't like," Jake says. Something uneasy settles over the room, but Kev smirks lightly to himself because Jake is always good with a comeback.

"Alright, that's enough, you two," Mrs. Brendar says audibly, while silently mouthing a thank you to Robert. "Does anybody know the answer to Jake's very astute observation?" She pauses before using the word astute. She is met with a chorus of gum snapping, writing utensils tapping impatiently, desks creaking, no anticipation or care for an answer, only an anticipation for leaving.

"Kevin, you've been quiet," Mrs. Brendar observes. "Do you have an answer to Jake's question?"

Looking up from his drawing, Kevin replies, "Um, those who fail to learn from history are doomed to repeat it?"

Smiling proudly at his answer, she thinks, at least she reached one kid this year. Not that anyone cared one way or the other what she was thinking.

"That's right."

Lifting a hand into the air, another student asks, "Can we go?" He drops his hand loudly back down to the desk.

"Yes, you can go. Remember, I know it's a holiday, but I want those vid screen reports logged! No exceptions! Robert, I want you to stay behind, the rest of you can go."

Notebooks are packed and chairs are scooted before she finishes her sentence.

Kev eyes Jake again and notices Jake's eyes have dark rings under them. His hair is combed neatly, but he had a habit of running his hand through his hair, which gives it a tousled look that girls would notice, but Jake didn't usually talk to any girls.

Kev was considered a brainy kid and there was a lot of

pressure on him to perform because one of his family line had gone AWOL, putting the entire family at risk. Kev was under threat of sterilization, as was every other member of his line as well.

He passed his tests and kept to himself. He answered questions politely and this had only ostracized him further. The only reprieve he was given by other students was that they knew he had no choice in how to behave. Kev was never razzed. He was never made fun of. He never allowed himself to cut up or be cut up, though some loose students he'd gotten to know at the University would jibe him in the ribs with an elbow and crack jokes. He knew they did it out of pity and sympathy, not friendship.

The students with Casted family lines, the ones who were fighting in the wars, mercilessly pegged him, but they did this to the others as well, so Kev was glossed over from real scrutiny most of the time. At least Kev's line had a shallow if dubious honor given to them, whereas the rest had none. A dubious honor to be sure, with a relative recently Casted then going AWOL. But it was better than no honor at all.

The students with Casted family lines, if they were the very best, would be Casted themselves, so they mostly targeted each other. The nickname they used for the other students in the University was "Fodder". Kev was never called "Fodder". He wasn't even allowed that.   He hadn't understood what it meant, but when he asked he was scorned for not knowing. After that, Kev decided to delve into history books to somehow try and earn the right for respect. Over time he came to realize since one member of his family had gone AWOL, his entire family line was 'muddy'.

Casted citizens going AWOL was one of the main reasons the wars were taking place. Kev would never have an opportunity to be Casted. For his family line he needed to prove his right to be "Fodder", which meant going above and beyond to be allowed anything close to a normal life. He would spend his time patching and fixing mistakes.

"Hey, Kenneth," Kev heard as he was leaving the main area of the University and heading towards a transit exit. He turned and noticed Jake walking beside him.

"It's Kevin," Kev said sullenly.

"Yeah, I know that," Jake says, dismissing Kev's assertion. "Let me see your U-card," he says.

"Why? What are you going to do with it?" A transit U-card was only good for a university student without implants. Years ago, one of the administrative officers of the University had explained to him that all U-cards were the same, aside from the unique signature of the person the card belonged to. After leaving the University, he would be fitted with implants depending on where he went.

"I want you to come to my place over the holiday," Jake says, giving Kev a quick smile. "I'm getting a few people together. No big deal."

"Really?" Kev reached into his pocket to pull out his U-card.

"Yeah, I got some old screens. We're going to dress up and play war, pretend we're not fodder, you know?"

"Okay." Handing over his U-card, Jake touches his key to the center of it.

"That's for tomorrow, see you soon." Handing the card back to Kev, Jake heads towards the transit doors.

Putting his U-card back in his pocket, Kevin heads through the scanner for his transit tunnel. The transit tunnels were heavily armored and barricaded but Kev had read the University ones were nowhere near as sophisticated as the ones that belonged to the other plantations.

Finding a seat in the transit car, it sped effortlessly through the tunnel back to Silverlake Terrace, the dorm where his family lived. When the transit car came to a stop in the middle of the terminal, the doors opened out on all sides, and Kev took his place waiting in line to have his card scanned. He didn't notice the other people in line, he was too elated. He'd been invited to another dorm, plus it was Jake Callen who invited him.

The card reader smiled. She'd been working as a card reader for Silverlake Terrace for a while and knew Kev to be a quiet kid. She noticed him and took the next card to scan.

Silverlake Terrace was an open dorm, made in the same

style as all the others in this arm of the Militia Wing plantation, the second plantation started on Earth. It was older but well protected. The top of the dome was airy and open and the sides of the walls had large, curved slats that could be closed in case of any type of chemical attack.

The floor of the dome allowed airflow from other parts of the planet, kept covered and protected for most of the day. Where the air came from would change and rotate automatically, unless a threat was detected.

Silverlake had a reputation for being an older and rundown dorm, but nothing could really be said to be clean after so much age and use.

In a large and open area, Kev made his way down the sidewalk towards his house. He had grown up in Silverlake Terrace, unable to leave until he was accepted to University when he turned 9, which was a little younger than most of the children. With Kev's aptitude and willingness to learn, combined with the condemnation of needing to redeem his family line, he was allowed to start at a young age. If someone did not pass aptitude by the age of 11, they were brought in to the University the following year without exception.

In his class, Kev was the youngest to pass his aptitude exams. He wasn't the youngest ever, there were others who had achieved similar distinction at the university. He was unusual, but not considered a rare commodity.

In the hierarchy of the school, the eldest were taught to be strong and to lead while protecting those behind them, who would learn over their shoulders. The front lines demonstrated what did or did not work.

Kev's mother, Linda, was proud of Kev for being accepted to University with the other children who were accepted at age 9. She understood Kev was not strong enough to earn his right as a true leader, but still felt a special pride he could one day be a leader of, at least, the youngest ones who were with him, though this had not, so far, proven to be the case.

She also knew time had a way of challenging and changing whatsoever made use of it, so Kev's mother was always able to see a special lining in Kev's life that would allow him to become what he needed to become.

When Linda heard Kev open the front door, she called out from the study. "Kev, I left a plate of cookies on the table for you, honey." She knew with the holiday coming, Kevin would hole up in his room and pour over history screens, technical manuals, and other random vid screens, learning as much as he could. He was quiet, and she loved him for his dedication.

Linda's family tended mostly towards artists and musicians, so the study contained several prized musical instruments. Kev's father, Albert, was a metal worker. He'd made advancements in engineering and designing in alloy and was heavily vaulted with the Armored Caste and had earned his right to have a child. Albert never shared with Kev which one of his relatives went AWOL, but explained to Kev if he demonstrated his usefulness and aptitude to others, the family line would soon be cleared.

He was strong with Kev, never lacking in discipline, but always ready with a heavy hand for praise to guide him in the ways of discipline and practice. This was how Albert managed to earn his right, and this is what initially attracted Linda to him.

Kev ran up the stairs to his room and shut the door behind him. Looking around the room that he spent most of his time in, he laid his bag next to his desk and called up a screen. He was only a member of three V-groups, and only at the University level, at least for now, anyway. He envied the others who were allowed to plug in directly, but he was satisfied that he was able to listen.

"Exciting news coming down the pipeline from the August Plantation in Asia, the Vision Caste has decided to open enrollment for chemistry students!"

A voice from inside the screen exclaimed, "Oh my gosh, Kev, that's us!"

While going through his things deciding what he should take tomorrow, he answered, "It is," loud enough to be heard over the rest of the announcement. The Militia Wing plantation was in the southern part of North America. The August plantation was the last plantation to open, an ocean away from where he was. The Vision Caste in the August Plantation had been maintaining order and prosperity for Earth's people as far back as Kevin could remember.

Kev was not the top student in the four universities by far but did excel in chemical theory. It was the one area he could focus on which took his mind away from everything and offered a chance at respect. Through effort, he managed to stay in the top rung, even if it was at the lowest level. The other students above him in testing and grading demonstrated more dedication and confidence. Kev's teachers felt the pressures put on him to avoid sterilization were hampering his abilities, but those were the breaks, he was lucky to be in the top tier at all.

Mandy spoke up again, "Are you going to apply?" Mandy was in the Armored Wing, a plantation far north, where Kev's father had made a name for himself before moving to the Militia Wing where Linda was located. The Militia Wing was home to the Warrior Caste. Mandy wasn't interested in the Warrior Caste but had struck up a bond with Kev because his father was known in the city she lived in.

Looking out the window, he considered his options. He was one of the lowest testers in the top tier and hardly stood a chance of standing out from his peers. He would have an easier time staying where he was.

"Oh, don't doubt yourself, Kev," Mandy said. "You should give yourself more credit. Grades aren't everything, you should know that. Besides, this is the Vision Caste looking for enrollment!"

Kevin thought perhaps being at the bottom sometimes showed the most opportunity for improvement.

"What are you going to do, Mandy?"

"I've already applied. I applied to 'Militia Wing City' too," she says and Kev thought he heard an almost faint and coy smile behind her words.

"Really?" he asks, struggling for his voice not to crack.

"Yeah, they're having enrollment too, you know, dummy."

Another voice rolls out on the screen. "And let me guess, Mandy, you want to know whether our poor boy Kev here is going to stay where he is now or go over and apply to the Vision Caste?"

"I'm just curious." Her voice comes through thicker and

sounds colored with covered and hidden emotions.

"And whatever happens, happens right?" Rodge says.

"Look, Rodge, I know Kev's a good guy who's got a tough break, but I'm not stupid. I'm going with whichever one gives me the better offer."

"Don't let your personal feelings destroy your chance at having a future and a life," Rodge reminds her.

Gritting his teeth, Kev is unable to contain the heat of his embarrassment.

"Where are you applying, Kev?" Rodge asks.

Kevin swallows, "I'll probably apply for the Vision Caste, too," though he hadn't applied for anything yet.

"Too? Where else have you applied?" Rodge asks.

Kev blinks back tears for a moment and is unable to come up with an answer.

"You're a fucking liar, Kevin. Good riddance," he laughs as Kev angrily reaches for the screen. "You are fucking worthless," he says getting in one last dig before the screen shuts down.

Sitting on the edge of his bed, the words played over and over in the silence of Kevin's mind. Rodge was just one of many who made his life miserable.

Seeing the blue and orange light start blinking on his desk, he pulled out his communicator to read the message.

Mandy's face was on the other end. "Hey, don't listen to Rodge, okay? He's just afraid you're going to do better than him because you've got so much to prove and you'll make him look bad even though he's smarter than you with this stuff. Keep your chin up, Kevin," she makes a little kiss in the air and waves before the message ends.

He didn't understand how he was supposed to do that. Dropping his communicator to the ground he buried his face in his hands on the edge of the bed. He'd been looking forward to tomorrow, but what was the point? He could try as hard as he could and never achieve what he wanted.

He fell asleep wondering why he wanted anything at all.

CHAPTER 11

Jake's house was located in the Ashlane Grotto dormitory and was a newer addition to the Militia Wing plantation. Construction had been finished within the last 20 years. Kevin took a transport to a connecting terminal and gave his U-card to the card reader.

The card reader scanned the card. "This is good for 10 more hours, the Callen's are being notified now," he says, entering a few commands into the screen. Kevin tucked the U-card into his pocket and looked at the card reader expectantly.

"The Callen family would like to know the purpose of your visit to Ashlane Grotto."

Trying to look confident in his answer, he replies, "I'm friends with one of the other students at the University."

The card reader adjusts the screen and hesitates.

"Jake Callen." Kevin says.

The card reader nods, "They've accepted responsibility, you have 10 hours."

Kev walked through the scanning tunnel slowly. After exiting, he realized he didn't know where to find Jake as the communicator in his pocket indicates a new message.

"Hey, glad you came." Jake says, followed by an open connection.

"Jake?"

"Yeah, where are you, Kev?"

"I just came in, where do I go?"

"Turn your beacon on."

Kevin lets out his location to anyone connected.

"Got it. To your left, you should see the woods, head that way," he says.

"Woods?"

"Yeah. We have trees, Kevin. We'll meet you there. Turn your full beacon on, I've got it tagged." Jake says.

Kev heads out. There were no trees in Silverlake. He takes a breath before straightening the fit of his light grey jacket, trying to act as if he'd grown up around trees his whole life and it would be completely normal to talk about them, or be around them, or use different words for them, no one would know how amazed he was by them, how taken aback he would be by how large they were and how they looked alive.

Just another part of this life where we would all die anyway.

He quickened his pace.

Soon enough, he heard low voices chattering and he headed towards them. He heard another laugh followed by more chatter. A branch snapped under Kevin's feet and the voices hushed quickly.

"Who's there?" he heard a female voice say.

He looked closer and could see Jake approaching him. "That's Kev, I invited him to come out."

"Who?" Another voice deeper than the first asks.

"Kev, he's from Silverlake. He's with Mrs. Brendar."

"Who?" the girl asks again.

"Don't be stupid," Jake says to the group.

Kevin puts his hands in his pockets and steps closer. "Hi," he says.

"I know him," the girl says. Kevin doesn't recognize her. "He was in my drawing class," she continues.

"That was a long time ago," Kevin says, trying to recognize her or recall her name.

"Where are we going, Jake? Why did you bring someone else?"

Turning to Kevin, Jake says quietly, "Don't worry, Rick's always like that, he still buys the story."

What story? Kevin thought.

Jake spreads his arms and pronounces with heavy sarcasm, "Rick, I brought Kevin here because he's a history buff and he's my new pal." He lays an arm around Kevin's shoulders and leaves everyone to try and figure out what was happening.

Rick crosses his arms and looks at both Kevin and Jake. The young girl, with blonde hair, gives Rick a glance while Kevin looks off at the interior wall of the dormitory in the distance, trying to hide that he is still marveling at the area. There's a moment of tension and the girl from Kevin's drawing class breaks out in a grin and Jake pats Kevin's shoulder.

"He knows more than you about what's going on," Jake says to Rick.

Suddenly, a voice is heard from behind them and they jump, alarmed.

"Are you guys ready?"

Jake motions for the group to follow.

"Where are we going?" Kevin asks Jake.

"Ethan knows how to look outside the dorm."

Kevin had never seen the world outside with his own eyes.

Ethan was stocky with long slicked and curled hair. "Why did you bring your boyfriend, Emily?" he says with a grin.

"Rick?" she asks and smiles, avoiding looking at Ethan. "Rick's going to the August Plantation, Eath. I'm staying here."

Jake points and the group notices a covered airflow unit. "It's down this way, Ethan." It was early afternoon, the dorm lights were low.

Passing a generator building with multiple signs posting hazards and warnings, Rick says, "Aren't any of you worried about sensors?"

Sighing, Jake turns towards Rick, "We're University, they don't have sensors out here that can see us. Besides, Ethan and I have already been out here. Nothing happened."

Rick stands still and says "Emily, I don't think this is a good idea."

She looks at Rick and then Ethan and Jake. "Why? Jake's right, the sensors can't see us. They're not looking for University out here."

"So? Will you explain that to them if we're caught?"

Ethan is already climbing the ladder on the side of the building and looks back at Jake.

"You coming, Jake?"

Jake waves a hand in the air and says, "Rick, you act like you are already Casted." He motions for Kevin to follow him.

Hesitating for a moment, Kevin nods and starts to follow Jake and Ethan up the ladder. Emily looks back between Rick and Jake, before following Kevin.

"Fuck," Rick says after a moment. He would not know how his parents would react to finding out that Rick was not accepted to the Vision Caste because it was discovered that he went outside of the city.

He decided to follow after them.

Standing on top of the main structure, they were still largely blocked from sight with the trees surrounding them.

Jake sits down and whispers, "We've got to stay low, we don't want anyone to see us," while Ethan crouches by the corner of the building looking outward. Night begins to descend over the dorm, as gradual as always. Rick looks over at Jake and is no longer filled with energy. "Is this safe, Jake?" he asks.

"Don't worry," Jake says, reassuring him, "Stay quiet."

"What's Ethan looking for?" Emily asks. Ethan waves his hand at them and continues looking out through the woods.

Kevin looks over at Emily and suddenly remembers seeing her in his drawing class, but they had never spoken. She catches him looking at her out of the corner of her eye and she grins at him.

"Jake, I'm serious!" Rick exclaims in hushed tones.

"Cool down, man," Jake says. "Do you want to live like this?"

"Like what?" He asks, not understanding the question.

"Come on, you know this is fucked," Jake says, waving his hand in the air.

"What? Air? Your hand? I know you're fucked, Jake, you don't have to tell me that!"

"No, I mean, they're lying to us! Kevin, how long have these dormitories been here?" Jake asks.

Kevin avoids looking at Jake. "Ashlane Grotto was finished

about 20 years ago."

"Right, what was before that?" Jake asks, quietly.

"What do you mean?" Kevin asks.

Rick turns to Kevin and says, "He's asking where we came from, he's always asking that."

"What, you mean our home planet?" Kevin asks.

Jake pulls a vial from his pocket and says "There's no such thing," and casually toys with it.

Rick looks at the vial. "What is that, Jake?" His voice deepens with fear.

"Wouldn't you want to know," he says and places the vial back in his pocket. "There's no such place as Avena, we never came from another planet, we come from this one."

"I believe it," Emily says.

Rick makes an attempt to control himself and Kevin realizes with dread that the conversation had entered a dangerous territory. You couldn't find any information about people being from Earth. Everyone knew Earth was the place where the Empire was being fought by the Anarchists because the Anarchists wanted to destroy all life, and the Empire was trying to get everyone back to Avena.

Anyone who made claims that people were from the Earth itself were worse than anyone and were of no help to anyone, they were deluded and dangerous. Earth was a dangerous place and it was poisonous. How could we have come from it? The Anarchists wanted to destroy all life on Earth because everything was so bad. Kevin looked at Jake again with a new perspective and began to regret his decision to throw caution to the wind.

"What do you think, Kevin?" Jake says.

Some dormant feeling in Kevin breaks loose. "There's nothing wrong with considering all possibilities," he replies.

Jake smiles. "That's right, good answer." He makes another attempt at giving Rick courage, "Don't worry, Rick. Come on." Ethan had signaled it was time to move forward.

Ethan motions for the group to get closer and points toward the covered airflow unit. "Okay, Jake and I found that you can open the airflow unit. There's a grate with a ladder we can climb down," he says.

"How do you know?" Kevin asks.

"The grate can open before the dorm lights turn all the way on at night and the unit isn't running. It's not locked."

"How can you see if it's running or not?" Rick asks.

Ethan says, "You can't from here. Come on, we don't have a lot of time."

They climbed down and made their way through a small tunnel that eventually opened out to a large walkway. An air flow exhaust could be seen in the distance and there was another tunnel to the right. It was fairly dark and only lit in sections.

"How did you find this?" Kevin asks.

Jake looks around and Ethan says "We were walking out in the woods and Jake got the bright idea to try and open the grate."

"How did you know you could open it?" Kevin asks.

Ethan says quietly, "My father works with the ventilation team for some of the dorms." He stops and turns to Kevin. "Jake says you're cool, but don't tell anyone. Our whole family can get in a lot of trouble and my Dad doesn't know I know about any of this."

Kevin raises his hands. "You're okay with me, I've never seen anything like this."

They continue walking and Jake holds up his hand. "Hold on."

"What is it?" Ethan asks.

He pauses for a minute, listening. "It's nothing, I thought I heard something, let's continue going."

As they continue walking, Rick asks Kevin, "Do you know where we are going? Seems like you know more about what's going on than I do, and I know these guys," he says, nervously laughing under his breath.

"I don't have any clue what's going on," Kevin says. "Jake invited me out here yesterday, he said he was having a group at his place for the holiday."

Rick looks puzzled. "Huh?" he says and continues walking nervously.

Emily comes in between the two while they are talking. "You looked upset when Jake said Avena wasn't real," she says to Kevin.

"Everyone knows we're here on Earth to get back to Avena. If it wasn't for the wars, we'd probably have the technology finished," Kevin says.

"Why do you think we're here, Kevin?" she says, touching him lightly on the shoulder and his heart beats faster.

"Um, it's a proving ground, like the Vision Caste says. We're here to get back to Avena."

"When do we get to go back?"

"When we build the technology that will get us back home and we stop fighting."

"What technology do we need?" she asks.

Kevin's memory is foggy. "They're talking about a large spaceship to carry everybody, there's research being done on a type of energy portal. It's confusing, the science screens are hard to understand."

"Did you ever think it wasn't true, Kevin?"

"What?"

"Did you ever consider that it could be a lie? That it's pretend? Where is Avena?"

Kevin begins to feel frustrated with her questions, although he didn't understand why. "Oh, this is all a lie that everyone is saying to each other. Avena is pretend and you're not pretending, is that right?"

She takes a step back from him and color seeps into her face. "You know the problem with you people who think you're so smart is that you really aren't smart at all. You're so easy to fool and manipulate."

The words sting him, but he rallies. "It's really hard to know what's right or wrong, or what will work or what won't," he says. "I've never thought about whether Avena was a real place or not," he says, but doubt tugs at the back of his mind and Emily seemed to be doing something to shape it.

"What drawing class did we have together, Kevin?" Emily asks.

"What?"

"What drawing class did we have together?" she asks again.

"Uh... Ms. Calloway?"

"I was never in drawing class, Kevin. I bet you wanted to believe we were in one together, though."

"What?" Kevin fumbles with embarrassment and a bright light suddenly floods the tunnel.

"Fuck!" Ethan says. Jake yells, "Get down!" and Ethan begins running back towards the entrance.

"Ethan!" Emily yells out and Rick grabs her.

"Let him go," Jake says.

Emily screams and pulls Rick's hands away and Rick lets her go. "What is going on?" she yells.

"Militia Wing and Empire City are about to be heavily bombed. Stay down, protect yourself," Jake says.

Emily starts scrambling to chase after Ethan and Rick grabs her again.

"How do you know that?" she says. "Ethan's going to get caught!"

"Trust me, we have to stay down here," Jake says.

A large screaming sound comes flying through the tunnel and the walls shake violently.

"Oh!" she yells.

Rick grips her tighter.

The walls begin to shake violently and with more force and loud pounding and scraping sounds are heard from above and they cover up their ears.

"What's going on?!" Kevin shouts to Jake over the noise.

"You wanted to prove yourself, mudder, now's your chance," Jake says.

"What?" Kevin yells.

"You're AWOL now, soldier."

"You're fucked!" Kevin yells and stands up, but is knocked to his feet as more of the area above is pounded by what sounds like a hail of large and heavy metal slamming into the dome above.

"Welcome to the war," Jake says, but no one hears him. Rick holds Emily close as she cries into his shoulder, sobbing and shaking. Kevin lays on the ground with his hands covering his head.

They wait as the sounds continue into the night. The curfew for Kevin's transit card is forgotten and a loud siren begins from the ground above.

CHAPTER 12

A low flying aircraft settles in the wreckage of one of the dorms of Militia Wing. It opens with a hatch that falls heavily to the ground. Four warriors of the Black Order step down the makeshift ramp and place a lozenge of gaze in their mouths.

They had originally been members of the Militia Wing as their musculature indicated, crafted by the handiwork of the Bio's Caste. The toolkit of old human genetics had been tweaked and modified to make them tougher, their elbows ended in curved bone that erupted from their calloused skin, ropes of modified bone growth twisting around their skeletal frames. They were an older generation of the modifications of the Bio's Caste and they had been alive for over 100 years.

There were still many of the original Warrior Caste left after all this time, but few bore those first scarrings proudly. These four did so as they had been among the first of any to defect to the Anarchists at the promise of a free immortality on Earth. They were wise to the lies and propaganda of the Vision Caste and believed there was no hope of getting mankind to Avena, and although most of the Anarchists still suspected they had descended from a mankind that had started someplace else, the years had ruined their memories. Why go back? Besides, the Empire held the secrets to gaze.

The lozenges they carried were slow acting and had been suited more towards the purposes of their new biology, allowing them several hours of constant regrowth.

"Split up, kill anything that stops you, tear apart anything you find, but make sure to leave as much as you can for salvage," Tomus said. "We're not supposed to meet any trouble, but take care of as much as you can. Turn on your vids so they will know what we're up against," he said melodically.

These four of the Black Order, a special order of the Anarchists, four of about 200 men altogether, had been fitted with an implant control that had been built and designed for safety and battle. This was new technology, done by the hands of slave engineers and the Bio's Caste themselves.

All recognizable information around them was transmitted to several locations because the Black Order proved to be some of the hardest warriors any of the castes had ever seen.

Dunley sucked on his lozenge and looked down at Tomus. Dunley was the tallest of the four and for good reason. He cocked his head to the side and sifted through the various sounds, listening for any arrhythmic sounds of life.

"Who wants dinner?"

Jackal and Metrim had already decided they would handle the destruction of most of the buildings and Dunley would keep an eye out for any signs of threat and end it quickly. Tomus would handle any aircraft.

"Come on, Metrim," Jackal says and the two head in different directions. Since the Anarchists had been unable to convince many of the Armored Caste to defect from the Empire and supply them with their substantial ability for siege manufacturing, the Black Order was rudimentary in their weaponry. They would salvage any material they could.

The aircrafts the Anarchists supplied to them were a boon and were powered by bacteria originally designed by the Bio's Caste. The aircrafts were stolen from Armored Wing itself.

The Anarchists wanted a strike against Militia Wing to rouse fear and support and convince more of the Warrior Caste to defect from the Empire. Members of the Warrior Caste were heavily divided in their loyalties in the war on Earth, and more and more of the Warrior Caste were turning to the Anarchists out of fear and support.

How the Anarchists had acquired the amount of artillery

needed for this raid, Dunley didn't know, but the city's shell had been cracked and the meat waited.

Tomus entered his mind and Dunley thought to him, "Why can't we see these little pigglies thinking anymore?"

"The Bios are quiet about it, maybe they helped the Empire breed it out of them."

Dunley spits on the ground. "Sad," he says.

"I don't want you to focus on questions, Dunley, I want you to wait for Empire, you got it?"

Dunley takes off with heavy and long strides and reassures Tomus. Circling an area where pigglie's seemed to be, he begins smashing his weapon against a domicile, shattering and breaking apart the encasement until they start to scream and panic.

He feels impacts hit his shoulder and back, and he staggers as another hits his neck and head guard.

"Shit." He closes his mouth tightly around the gaze lozenge and tries to dig the metal out of his shoulder before his skin heals. He dives behind nearby wreckage and continues digging deeper for the projectiles. He takes his helmet off and stretches a mouth guard around his mouth so his lozenge will not accidentally fall out.

A voice comes in through one of his implants. "You've got an hour. Keep moving, don't worry about the bullets, just get as many of them out of their houses as you can."

He has no way to communicate back but does as he's told. He slams his weapon against anything that will bust loudly, creating as much noise as he can. More projectiles land nearby, targeting him, and another explosion goes off in a different part of the area.

"It's hard to do this when you're only one person," Dunley thinks. He quickly heads back out from the wreckage and several of the pigglies are amassing together. He still can't see their minds.

Switching tactics, he approaches them cautiously, just enough with their body rhythm to keep them confident enough as they prepare to fire more shots. Sensing the timing, he lunges at them and knocks one back while grabbing another. He drags it out into the center of the street as the rest of them fall away. He throws the piggly to the ground and lays his mace down several times into its head and body.

"There," he thinks. "Can't be everywhere at once. Flee, pigglies. Flee."

Another siren starts blaring. The pigglies have noticed the dorm walls have been destroyed and several are making their way out through the shattered and broken metal walls. Dunley chuckles. Some of them see the bodies in the street and turn and run in other directions.

Sensing Metrim nearby, Dunley looks through his eyes. Metrim is making short work of various structures with a powered jackhammer.

"How much time do we have?" Metrim asks.

"We're supposed to be here less than an hour and then come back and finish," Dunley says. They both have two hours until the healing stops.

"Alright, let's keep moving," Metrim says.

"Dunley, get over to Tomus, he's north of you," Dunley hears over his implant. He makes his way back to the aircraft and sees several slaves of the Militia Wing and Tomus is fighting to keep them away.

"Alright," Dunley thinks, and chuckles again, sucking on the lozenge. The mace at the end of the metal shaft whistles loudly and it is difficult to hear through all the noise, but Dunley has taught himself to listen for it and listen to it sing.

A few of the slaves fall and the rest give over quickly and run for whatever safety can still be found. There is a pain Dunley feels that he can't shout after them, letting them know there is nowhere to run, they have been defeated and there is no hope for them, anywhere, but he has gotten used to this type of painful silence.

"Any Empire?" Tomus asks in Dunley's mind. He is wearing a mouth guard and a helmet as well.

"No, but they should be coming."

Tomus cocks his head.

"They've changed the plan, we need to leave. Jackal and Metrim have already been informed. Come on, the pilot is ready."

Tomus and Dunley head into the aircraft and Metrim and Jackal are not far behind. The bay door is pulled up to the side of the vehicle and after a few minutes, the aircraft lifts into the air.

Tomus removes his helmet and mask. Metrim goes to do the same, but Tomus waves him down.

"Not yet," he says. "We've done our part, but they need us somewhere else. The salvage group will be heading out this way."

Dunley takes off his gear, regardless of what Tomus had said, and lets out a satisfied breath.

"At last," he says.

Metrim thinks, "Why did they cut us short?"

"Not sure," Tomus says.

A message is received through their implants, "Empire City is under attack."

Jackal says, "What?"

"We're pulling you out. You're going to regroup with the other members of the Black Order. We were only after the Militia Wing. Empire City is under threat, possibly by the Grippers."

Metrim thinks "That's good, right?"

"It's not expected," Jackal thinks.

Tomus pauses a minute and says, "We can put pressure on the Empire to turn over the secret of gaze."

Jackal voices, "I guess they want us to hit them hard and put it on them."

Dunley nods in agreement. The implant continues.

"We are moving the fleet south to Empire City, but it will take several hours. When you arrive, everyone will pull together and await orders."

Metrim finally takes off his helmet and mask. "That's all of us?" he says loudly. "They're bringing us all there?"

"Looks like it," Jackal thinks.

"What are they going to have us do?" Metrim says.

"Kill the Grippers, then attack Empire City, that's what I'd assume," Tomus thinks. "It makes sense. The Empire's weak now, we kill the Grippers, then attack Empire City, the Empire will be forced to turn the secret over to us."

"What about Armored Wing? What about the Armored Caste?" Metrim says.

"Fuck Armored Caste," Dunley says.

"I'd like to see you take that mace of yours to a tank," Jackal says.

"This might not be wise," Tomus says. "The Armored Caste have always been loyal to the Empire."

"How did the Grippers attack Empire City?" Jackal thinks, uneasily.

Dunley eyed the viewport and gave a long look to the lights streaming by. It would be a hot, long night of gaining the upper hand, ending with a bid for the prize of the Empire. The Black Order would surely drive itself as a wedge between the Empire and it's salvation, rightfully positioned as the most powerful of all.

"Come on, come on," Jake said under his breath. He sat with his back against a wall, hunched over his knees and nervously running his fingers through his hair again and again. The group had fallen asleep long after the noise above had become quiet.

Rick opens his eyes. After a long look at Jake, he asks, "What are you waiting for?" Kevin begins stirring in his sleep and shifts his pack under his head.

"We're supposed to stay down here until someone comes and gets us," Jake says.

"Did you sleep?" Rick asks. After a moment, he rubs his eyes and looks at Jake again, angrily. "Who's supposed to get us, Jake? How did you know about any of this?"

"Someone is going to come and get us out of here," Jake says, repeating himself.

"Who? How did you know this was going to happen?" Rick gets to his feet and looks down at Jake.

"We're slaves," Jake says. "Avena and Casted? The Empire is using us, and lying, too."

Heat and anger wells behind Rick's eyes. "The Empire is

lying to us, Jake?" Trying to fight back tears, he says, "My family is dead! Did you hear that? Is that a lie? They're all dead up there because the Empire is lying to us?" Lunging at Jake, he tries to grab on to him and Jake scrambles away.

"Listen to me!" he yells. "It's a lie! None of it's real! They are lying to us, all of them!" Scrambling to get to his feet, Rick pushes him down and hits him in the face.

"Everyone's dead, Jake!" Feeling his anger overflow, he lands another blow and Jake struggles to get away.

"Rick, you have to believe me!" Jake pleads. Rick hits him again. Jakes chokes and starts to cry. "Will you please listen to me?" he says, sobbing.

"No! It's people like you who caused this to happen!"

Tears well up in Rick's eyes and his anger is passing. His voice is hoarse and he struggles to catch his breath while Jake coughs and tries to get up.

"What are you doing?" Kevin yells.

Rick's arms and hands begin shaking and he sits down. Jake has blood running down his face from his nose and his eye is beginning to swell.

"Are you alright?" Kevin asks him. He kneels down, grabs Jake's hand and helps him up.

Emily takes a pouch of water from her bag. "Do you have a towel or a shirt or anything?" she asks Kevin.

"Yeah, I've got another shirt, hold on." He walks over to his bag and pulls out a shirt.

"You came prepared," she says.

"I thought I might be able to stay longer," Kevin says.

Pouring water over the shirt, she cleans some of the blood from Jake's face carefully. Jake takes the shirt and wipes at his face and neck.

Rick is still sitting down and shaking. Finally getting himself back under control, he looks up. "I'm sorry. I shouldn't have lost it like that, Jake."

Jake tries to grin, but it's shaped more like a grimace. He continues cleaning his neck and is angry. Kevin looks at Rick.

"What are we supposed to do now, Jake?" Rick asks.

"We're waiting for someone to come get us," Pushing

gently around his face, he feels it beginning to swell.

"Who? Anarchists?" Rick says and he clenches his fists and drops his hands, realizing what he's doing.

"No," Jake says. He turns to Kevin, "Do you know anything about the Grippers and how they're trying to free Earth, and everyone on it, from the wars?"

"I've never seen anything about 'Grippers'. I know we're not supposed to stay on Earth, I mean," he waves his hand around and tries to muster up some humor. "Look at this place."

"He's right, Jake," Rick says. "I don't know if I believe everything the Vision Caste says, but you can tell that something's not right. I'm not doing anything to help the Anarchists."

Kevin says to Rick, "The Anarchists are Casted that defected from the Empire."

Rick's eyebrows raise, "Really?" he says.

Kevin turns back around and clenches his fists a few times. "Well, yeah. The Anarchists think it's better to stay on Earth and not go back to Avena. That's why they're trying to stop the Empire."

"It's a lie," Jake says.

"Shut up, Jake," Rick says angrily.

"I agree with him, Rick," Emily says.

"Why are we fighting, then?" Rick says. "Why are people dying?"

"It's the immortality," Jake says.

"What 'immortality'?" Rick asks.

"Casted can't die, or they can't die easily. Some of the Casted have been alive for centuries," Jake says. "I haven't been told a lot."

"So they are immortal, that's what I thought," Kevin says.

"What do you mean?" Rick asks.

"There's some kind of medicine you can take that will make you live a long time, you won't die and it heals you," Jake replies.

"I haven't heard about a medicine, but I was pretty sure the Casted could become immortal," Kevin says.

Rick looks at Emily. "Why do you believe Jake?"

"Because he's right. We're from Earth. This is our world," she says.

"I can't believe that," Rick says.

"I know you can't, Rick," she says.

"Why can the Casted become-- immortal?" Rick says.

"It might be from Avena," Kevin says. "If you read the screens enough, sometimes they change. There was something I read about the Anarchists wanting to have immortality on Earth, and that was why they were fighting the Empire, but I couldn't find anything about it again."

The rhythmic scraping sound starts to slow down. Rick stands up quickly and backs away. "What is that?"

"I think it's an exhaust," Kevin says.

"It is," Jake says. "Come on, that's us."

"Wait, who are we waiting for?" Rick asks.

"I don't know who, but it's the Grippers. Come on," he says.

"No! I don't know anything about 'Grippers' and I'm not going with you, Jake," Rick says.

"Would you rather be dead?" Jake asks while holding the shirt under his nose. "Come on," he says again and starts walking. With no other good options, the group begins to follow him.

They arrive to see the large blades have stopped. Jake pulls down the handle of the door next to it, dead without electricity, and a large latch clicks and it opens.

A blinding light shines and it is difficult to see behind it. "You Jake?" a voice asks.

"Yeah," Jake says. "I've got some friends with me."

"Okay then, 'Jake'. Drink the vial."

Jake reaches into his pocket and removes the vial and twists the cap off.

"Who kicked your ass, kid?" the voice observes.

"A friend of mine," Jake says and tips the vial back and drinks the liquid inside.

"Good choice in friends," the voice says. The light swivels a little and Kevin realizes it's attached to something.

"Your friend Jake is about to drop down cold, I suggest you

carry him to the vehicle," the voice says.

"What?" Rick says loudly into the darkness.

"Oh god," Jake says and begins shivering as he drops the vial. He doubles over and clutches his stomach in pain.

"Jake?" Rick asks nervously, while Jake begins to shake. "What the hell is wrong with him?" he asks, as Jake doubles over on to the floor.

"It's the quickest and best tracking agent we could find, but he's going to be hurting a lot while it runs through his system. Come on, bring him here," the voice says.

Jake's eyes roll back in his head and his hands are trembling and his body is shaking. Kevin grabs his legs and Rick grabs his shoulders and they carry Jake forward as the light is moved to follow them.

"Who's the girl?" the voice asks.

"She's my friend," Rick says. "Leave her alone."

"Emily," Emily says.

The light swivels back to the door and then upward and bounces from the ceiling, illuminating the area. A large, open vehicle is seen and Kevin recognizes it as some type of transport, but a military one. A dark-haired man is handling the spotlight attached to the upper frame of the vehicle.

"Name's Aaron. It's a pleasure to meet you. Put him in the back seat and stay with him, we're going to need to get out of here."

Kevin looks over at Aaron as Rick helps him get Jake into the back seat. Jake is slumped over and Aaron says, "He won't be unconscious for long."

"You look like us," Kevin remarks. He had expected Aaron to at least have implant scars. "How do you know Jake?"

"Let him tell you," Aaron says. He walks over to the back of the vehicle and pulls out a length of rubber cable with metal clamps on the end. "We need to make sure he doesn't fall out of the vehicle," he says, and hands the rubber cable to Rick. Rick pulls the length of it apart and looks at Aaron trying to understand how to tie Jake down with it. He looks at Kevin and says "Can you help me?"

"Yeah," Kevin says.

"Emily, you ride up front with me, we need these two to stay in the back and keep Jake down," Aaron says.

"No, Emily's staying in the back with me," Rick says.

"That's fine," Aaron says.

"I'll ride up front," Kevin says to Rick.

After Aaron sits behind the vehicle's controls, Kevin climbs into the seat next to him. Aaron reaches over and opens a compartment in front of Kevin. A pistol is seen on the compartment door.

"You know how to work one of these?" Aaron asks.

"No," Kevin says.

"Good," Closing the door, he reaches into his pocket and pulls out an electronic key.

"You know how to use a key?" Aaron asks.

"Yes," Kevin says.

"Okay," Aaron says and puts the key back into his pocket. He adjusts a mirror and looks back at Rick and Emily. "Is Jake alright?"

"I think so, we couldn't tie him down," Rick says. "How did you know we were going to be attacked?"

"Hold on to him," Aaron says and presses the pedal down. "I'll answer your questions later." He looks at Kevin and then to the backseat. "We have about three hours of fuel if we do this right. Jake's bloodstream is pumping out a heavy signal, it won't take that long for us to be found."

Aaron is slowly driving the vehicle through a large tunnel.

"How are we going to get out of here?" Rick asks.

"This tunnel opens out to a reservoir. I don't think the Empire expected anyone to find it, or to dismantle the security," Aaron says. "Kevin, I'll need you to get out and pull up a roller door when we get to it and then hop back in."

"What?"

"If you haven't noticed, there's no power around us. You'll need to manually pull up the roller. There's a handle on the bottom of it, just pull up as hard as you can, the weight will catch it, and it'll open. It's not locked."

"What is going to happen?" Emily asks.

"We're going to get out of here," Aaron says.

"How fast does this thing go?" Kevin asks.

Aaron looks at the console behind the wheel. "Pretty fast."

The vehicle eventually maneuvers to the area Aaron had indicated earlier.

Kevin pulls up the roller door and the morning sunlight blinds him. He holds his hand over his face, surveying the landscape and an old and terrible smoke hangs in the air. The smell is not quite like anything Kevin had ever experienced before. The sky is such a deep blue that Kevin stumbles.

"Get back in the car!" Aaron yells.

Kevin tears himself away and climbs into the passenger seat.

"There's a strap next to you, you need to pull that across your body. There's a place to latch it on the other side."

Rick and Emily look around. Jake is shivering and sweating. "We don't have one of those!" Rick says as he hears a click from Kevin's seat.

"Find something to grab," Aaron yells. The vehicle's tires spin loosely, then gain traction and they hurtle up an incline and land in the dirt.

"Hold on!" Aaron shouts.

Kevin notices in the distance the wreckage of Militia Wing. "Oh no," he says.

"No one needs to look at it," Aaron says. "There's nothing we can do about it."

"What?" Kevin says. He looks back and notices there are people and they have spotted the vehicle speeding off.

"Hey, there are people still alive!" Rick says.

"There's nothing we can do for them. Hold on tight."

"But we need to help them!" Rick says.

"There's nothing we can do, kid, okay?" Aaron looks through the mirror and Emily, Kevin and Rick turn to watch people running after them. Aaron presses the pedal harder and the vehicle accelerates. The people behind them slowly stop running.

"Take us back!" Kevin yells.

"They're going to die. We only knew Militia Wing would be attacked about two days ago. We didn't have anything to do with this. I can't take you back. Trust me, you're better off with me right now."

CHAPTER 13

The The sun shone high in the sky over a long and low grassland area. The trees spread and arced their limbs through the atmosphere, soaking in the oxygen, or the nitrogen, or the carbon dioxide or the warmth and the pressure of the blanket of air that slipped through the branches and moved the leaves in the wind.

"Where are we headed?" Kevin asks.

"We're on our way to meet someone who lives out here," Aaron says. The vehicle speeds down a fragmented and broken highway. The stark and flat landscape stretched for miles, broken only by an occasional lone tree or patch of tall grass mixed with weeds. From a distance, Kevin is able to make out a few details, but as they approach, they move by him, a phenomena of which he had no prior context.

Aaron looks over at Kevin. "Just keep your head up, okay?"

Kevin looks back at the others. Jake is lying calmly with his head in Emily's lap and is a ghastly mix of white and green. Emily has her eyes closed and is leaning on Rick's shoulder. Rick has a hand to his face and is looking off into the distance. His other hand rests idly on Jake's leg. The group was subdued with the events unfolding.

"You grew up in there? 'Dorms', you said?" Aaron asks Kevin. Kevin looks back at Aaron and Aaron looks back at the road.

"Yeah, we all did," Kevin says. He tries to sit comfortably

like the others but is unsuccessful.

"My name is Aaron, by the way, I don't know if I mentioned that."

"Kevin."

"Kevin, it's nice to meet you. It shouldn't take too long to get where we are going. Just relax for now."

Kevin rests back in his seat. "The sun is really bright."

"Yeah, it is. Don't look at it," Aaron says and laughs under his breath.

"I wasn't, I just didn't realize it was so open. I don't feel comfortable."

"Well, I couldn't imagine growing up in one of those places, so we're even there," Aaron replies.

"How far are we going?"

"What do you mean?" Aaron says.

"How big is it out here?"

"Uh, it's pretty big. Militia Wing is in Texas, but a lot of people don't know what that means. Let's put it this way, if we kept driving like this for a while, there would still be days left, even at this speed."

Kevin folds his hands together and turns in his seat trying to lie back and be comfortable.

"You can move the seat back," Aaron says.

"Who's going to find us out here?" Kevin asks. He doesn't tilt his seat back, it makes him uneasy to even think about it.

"There's a man out here by the name of," he pauses, "Kristof. He has some kind of tracker that will spot Jake. He should be able to see us when we reach the rest stop and he's going to take us where we need to go from there."

"Where are we going after that?" Kevin asks.

Aaron looks down at the console. "I'm not sure. Don't worry, for now, all of you will be alright. I'm sorry I can't answer your questions better."

Kevin blinks and looks back at Aaron. "What?"

"I mean, you've probably got a lot of questions. I couldn't possibly answer all of them," Aaron says.

Kevin closes his mouth realizing Aaron has answered every question he'd asked.

"I can't imagine what it's like being in there, but your friend Jake got you out, he made a good choice," Aaron says.

"Are you Grippers?" Kevin asks, feeling awkward.

"Yeah," Aaron says.

"Are you Casted?"

"What?" Aaron says, giving Kevin a confused look.

"Are you Casted?" Kevin asks him again.

"I don't know what you mean. Am I in the Empire?"

Kevin pauses. "Yeah," he says.

"No. Do you mean, can I heal?"

Kevin's stomach churns and his heart beats quickly. "Yes, can you die?"

"That's a tough question, Kevin. Why don't you ask me a different one?"

"Are you in the war?" Kevin says.

"There's not really a war. The Empire is fighting a war with itself. We're the guys who know what's going on when a lot of people out here don't,"

"Are you from Earth?" Kevin asks.

"What?" he says, making a heartfelt attempt to laugh lightly.

"Do you know about Avena?" Kevin asks. Aaron looks over at Kevin and Kevin's eyes are wide.

"The other planet?" Aaron asks and looks worried.

"Yeah," Kevin says and nods quickly.

"I don't know about Avena, but I've heard about it," Aaron says. "Why do you ask?"

"Mankind is supposed to be from Avena," Kevin says.

Aaron runs his fingers over his mouth and mutters.

"That's why I was asking if you were from Earth, that's what Jake was saying," Kevin says.

"You mean here? Yeah, I'm from here, I was born here," Aaron says.

"No, that's not what I--" Kevin stops speaking.

"Don't worry about that stuff right now, okay, Kevin? Here's the important part. You're going to know a lot of stuff the people you will meet don't know and that's really important. The best thing you can do is to listen a lot and try to answer questions as simply as you can, without saying a lot, okay?"

Kevin suddenly realizes he is not going to see his family again and is suddenly afraid to look at the others behind him who he doesn't know at all.

"How old are you, Kevin?" Aaron asks.

"I'm 16," he says absently. Aaron looks over and Kevin's eyes are still wide.

"That's pretty cool, huh? Teenager?"

"What?"

"You're a teenager, that's gotta be cool, right?"

"I don't know what that means," Kevin says.

Aaron sits back with his hand on the steering wheel and rubs his face and chin for a bit.

"Alright, Kevin, look, I'm going to be square with you. We're heading to meet with a guy who stays out here, close to Militia Wing, the place where you're from. He's very protective of where he lives because he helps us get gaze. Do you know what gaze is?" Aaron asks.

"No," Kevin says halfheartedly.

"Gaze is some kind of medicine the Empire makes in its plantations. Militia Wing is one of those plantations. I've never met anyone born in one of them, so I don't know what you do or don't know."

"I know what a plantation is," Kevin says.

"Good, because I don't, Kevin," Aaron says.

It's quiet for a while and Kevin breathes uneasily. "Can we stop this thing? I don't feel well."

"I can't stop, I'm sorry, just try and breathe deeply and stay calm, or hold it, or whatever is wrong, it shouldn't take much longer," Aaron says. "You might want to try just kind of lightly looking around, try putting your hand out in the wind."

"There are three plantations," Kevin says after some time.

"There's a big one in Asia, right?" Aaron asks.

"That's the August Plantation," Kevin says. He thinks to mention the Vision Caste and then realizes that it might not be a good idea to say any more to whoever this is, not knowing who they were, even if they were the person who had given the advice to begin with.

Trying to avoid thinking how he spent the day before, wondering if he could be accepted at the August Plantation, he stares out in the distance. Finally, he realizes what took place earlier was what the Vision Caste was fighting against.

"The August Plantation is the religious center, right?" Aaron asks.

"Religious?" Kevin asks, feeling confused by the conversation.

Aaron balks. "That's where the idea of other planets is coming from?"

"Don't you know about Avena?" Kevin asks.

"No. Some of the Empire are talking about being from other planets, it didn't start happening until recently," Aaron says.

"Avena is where we're all from, but we need to find a way to get back," Kevin says.

"Pretend I don't know anything, Kevin,"

"We're originally from Avena, but we were left here on Earth because of the wars, so we're supposed to get back to Avena. Even the Vision Caste doesn't know how, they say somehow Avena watches over us and will show us where to find the planet again and how to get back to it, but it won't happen until the wars are over, or we find a way to get back ourselves,"

Aaron sits back and thinks awhile. "So we're not from Earth, then?" he says finally.

"No, we can't be, because Earth is so dangerous," Kevin says.

"Is that what you believe?" Aaron asks.

"What do you mean?" Kevin says.

"Weren't you born here?" Aaron says.

"Yes," Kevin says. "It was our ancestors who came from Avena."

"I see. So if the wars stop, we get to go back," Aaron says.

"Yes," Kevin says. "The Anarchists are trying to keep us here on Earth and that's why we're having these wars," He realizes Aaron might not know about the Anarchists at all, yet he believed people were from Earth. Kevin started to grasp what the Vision Caste was fighting against.

"The Anarchists left the Empire, that's why the wars are

happening," Kevin says.

"You think I'm with the Anarchists, Kevin?" Aaron asks.

"No," Kevin says and pauses. "But you don't know what's going on."

"So, if I say that I want to be here on Earth, I'm with the Anarchists?"

Kevin thinks a minute. "Without knowing," he says quietly.

The highway from Militia Wing is remarkably free of debris. Aaron notices an old and rusted vehicle off to the side and slows down, nervously checking the mirror facing behind him.

"Alright, Kevin, we're going to be stopping soon. How are you two back there? How is Jake?"

Rick stirs out of sleep and Emily says, "He's alright, he's sweating a lot."

"We need water," Rick says.

"No problem," Aaron says. "We're going to stop soon and wait. There's a rest stop coming up, that means that we're going to get off of this highway."

Emily looks at Rick. "Are we going to be able to walk around?" Rick says to Aaron.

"Yeah, don't worry, we should be safe," Aaron says.

"How soon?" Emily asks.

"Soon, not long," Aaron says.

I can't believe you, Jake, Rick thinks. Jake had never caught on to how much Emily liked him, or anyone. He probably didn't even care what happened to anyone who liked him, he never noticed. Rick was having a difficult time because he knew people from his dorm were still alive.

"Are you going to take us back?" Rick asks.

"I don't know what's going to happen. I'm supposed to bring Jake and whoever is with him to the man we're about to meet. His name is Kristof, and I haven't met him before, but he's waiting for Jake," Aaron says.

Slowing even more, Aaron finally spots the turnoff to the rest area and pulls over. The group slowly exits the vehicle as birds are seen off in the skyline.

"Is that why Jake joined you?" Emily asks.

"Possibly," Aaron replied.

"Why did you join?" she asked.

"I know about gaze. I'm not with the Empire, so I didn't have a choice," Aaron said.

Rick walked up to Kevin who was sitting away from the vehicle on debris that might have been a bench a long time ago.

"How are you doing? I'm sorry Jake got you into this," Rick says.

"It's alright," Kevin replies.

"No, it's not alright. Jake is always doing this. He doesn't care about anyone, he doesn't think about what he says or does and what it means to people and what it does to them."

Kevin is silent for a while.

"I don't even know if we're going to get back home!" Rick says. "I don't know what is going to happen, there were people still alive."

"That's true," Kevin says, faintly.

"What dorm were you in?"

"Silverlake," Kevin says.

"That's one of the older ones, right?"

Kevin says, "I don't want to talk about this right now."

"I know, but I looked back, I've never seen the city from outside. It was a wreck, but it wasn't all gone. Maybe Silverlake didn't get attacked," Rick says.

"Maybe," Kevin says, vacantly.

"I care, Kevin. I know Jake doesn't, but I do. Don't listen to this crap about what's going on out here. You know as well as I do that we didn't do this to ourselves," Rick looks off. "'The Empire is fighting itself', can you believe it? You know it wasn't the Empire that attacked us, we're not attacking ourselves."

"I didn't think we were," Kevin says softly.

Rick looks around and leans closer to Kevin. "I'm going to get back and help in the city, whatever they need. Emily is probably going to try and go with Jake, but I know her, she won't leave her family behind for long." He looks around to see if anyone can hear him. "I hope we never see Jake again, and if we do, I… I don't know what I'd do, Kevin."

Kevin hears a darkness in Rick's voice. It's hollow with a faint resoluteness lost somewhere within, a small metal tree standing firm without ground inside the hollow void.

"I don't ever want to see him again," Rick says. The sound is hollow, but the faint steel branches do not waver.

"Okay," Kevin says faintly again as his eyes begin to tear.

The hollow sound becomes heavy with emotion, "I have to get Emily to come back with us."

The metal tree fades into the void, but Kevin can still hear it as it echoes. He turns his head and looks over at the vehicle and Emily is still speaking with Aaron. It seemed as if Aaron was emphatically explaining something to her and Kevin could see she was torn inside.

"She won't forgive you if you get angry with Jake," Kevin says.

"Yeah. She won't listen to me," Rick says. "I'm just going to stay quiet and find a way for us to leave. Jake might help, he doesn't care about her."

"What do you think gaze is?" Kevin asks.

"I don't know, you know how the city is," Rick says.

"Do you think there is such a thing?"

"I don't know," Rick says. "You said there were screens about people that couldn't die?"

"The screens change if you watch them enough. I thought the Casted couldn't die, and then that's what Jake said. Aaron said the same thing and said it was something called 'gaze' and it's from the plantations. He says it comes from our cities."

Rick looks at Kevin sidelong when he says 'our'. He pauses and says finally, "Whatever it is, I don't want these guys to have it."

Emily turns towards the two. "Rick?" she says, and he gets up from the bench and Kevin follows him.

"Aaron said he's a part of a group called the 'Grippers', and they're trying to protect the people out here from what the Empire is doing. Jake is trying to join them," she says.

Rick looks over at Aaron. "What exactly is it that the Empire is doing, Emily?" Rick asks.

Her eyes narrow. "He said the Empire is making something

called 'gaze' and people won't die if they have it."

"What's wrong with that?" Rick says.

"He also said they're fighting each other and killing the people on Earth," Emily continues.

Rick's face turns red. "How do you know that? How do you know he's telling you the truth?" Making an effort to keep his anger with Emily in check, he bites back words he could use, even her own words to use against her, but they are left unsaid.

"Why is he going to lie about that, Rick?" she says quietly.

Rick's anger subsides a little and he says, "How do you know he's not against us?"

"Why would he be?" she says.

Rick throws his hands outward. "So what are you going to do, Emily? You're going to go out here and do what? Stop it? You're going to stop all this?" he says. She doesn't answer him. He throws his hands up and points at Aaron and Emily.

"What's the point? What is he going to do? What are you going to do? I didn't attack our city. I didn't start the wars, I don't want them to happen! I'm not trying to make them happen! I don't know anything about what he is saying, and he is saying we're the problem and we were the ones that were attacked!"

"We didn't attack your city," Aaron says.

Rick's voice still wavers. "Someone did," he says finally.

"We had nothing to do with it," Aaron repeats. He stands still, looking at Rick and waits. His hands are calmly at his sides.

"I'm not going to believe anything you say," Rick says.

"That's fine. I'm not asking you to," Aaron replies.

"How much longer are we going to be out here?" Emily asks, but she continues looking at Rick.

Aaron shoots her a grin out of habit. He had started to worry about how to feed the teenagers or where to take them if Kristof did not arrive. The possibility had not been discussed because no one would know what to do if it happened. Rio was a longer distance than the teenagers might be comfortable with, and he would need to let the others in Rio know Kristof hadn't arrived as soon as he could. He would need to wait several days in this area to make sure Kristof would or would not arrive and was at a loss for what to do in the meantime.

The tracking agent Jake had been given would last about a day and would be detected by the equipment Kristof had with him. It would let him know Aaron and Jake survived the attack and where to find them soon after. In any event, everything was arranged for meeting at this rest stop. Beyond a day, Kristof was supposed to eventually arrive.

"A few more hours," Aaron says.

They heard a sound in the distance. A large, white armored vehicle was approaching from the highway.

"Hey, that's an XLM transport!" Kevin says.

Aaron turned to look in the direction Kevin was facing. The vehicle's windows were dark. A large crack ran across a window in front. The white plastic covering of the transport tapered to a wedge and its six wheels traveled slowly.

"That's Kristof," Aaron said with relief.

"That's an XLM transport, it's from Armored Wing!" Kevin says.

"It's Kristof," Aaron repeats.

The XLM pulls off of the highway into what Aaron had called a rest stop. It stops in front of the group and the body of the vehicle lowers and covers the wheels.

"If it's Armored Caste, we can get back," Rick says.

"Look, it doesn't matter," Aaron states. He pulls his jacket back slightly, and casually, in case he needed to reach for the plastic gun he had strapped to his side, and signal he carried a weapon in the event it had been detected.

Hearing the latch move, the side of the vehicle pushes forward and slides back from the front. A robotic arm moves with precision and metallic and rubberized fingers grasp the edge of the opening. A figure clad in white plastic body armor steps down from the vehicle. The joints of the knee are exposed with a flexible material and the plastic armor surrounding the shins tapered outward slightly at the top.

Kristof's chest is covered and encased in more of the plastic material. The area on both sides of his abdomen reveal open and crisscrossed slats and above this is white, thick, and protected. The robotic hand at the end of his mechanized right arm swivels and the fingers compress into the slats, grasping and hooking on to the armor and the arm remains still.

The helmet he wears is white and bullet-shaped with a red cross on the forehead. A clear visor covers his face and colors are seen shifting and changing in the visor as he moves his head.

"I want you three to go over to the vehicle," Kristof says. He looks over at the three from the University and some of the shapes in the visor slow to a stop and the colors blink slowly. "By-- Jake," Kristof says.

Aaron heads briskly inside of the transport as Kristof begins walking around the area. The metallic and rubberized fingers of his right hand reach into one of the slats and he presses a button inside. The colors leave the visor and he uses both hands to remove the helmet.

His hair is soft and long, white and grey. His face is tanned and dark. His mustache is long and trimmed, his beard is not. His face looks much older than Aaron's.

Kristof turns and looks at the children. "Don't worry," he says. "You're in better hands than you realize."

They stand close to each other. Emily and Rick lean into each other, no longer able to hide from themselves the depth of caring and solace they provide one another, as fear and reality begin to strip them back. Emily trembles slightly, not from pain but from emotion, and Rick's face is white and he weakly asks if Kristof is from the Armored Caste. Kevin nods but looks off into the distance.

"No," Kristof says. He doesn't look back at them but instead watches as Aaron leaves the transport with a container.

"We're going to sort this out," Kristof continues. "Aaron, I want you to follow behind." Kristof turns back to the others. "I don't care which of us you ride with. You're free to ride with me," he says.

"Jake drank that tracking agent about 4 hours ago," Aaron says.

The three teenagers begin to calm as Kristof and Aaron speak.

"He seems to be doing alright," Aaron says and looks over

at the vehicle. "I don't know what it's supposed to do to him."

"Rick, let me stay with Jake," Emily says quietly.

"Do you want me to stay with you?" Rick asks her.

"No," she says.

Rick turns and looks at Aaron.

"I'll be alright, Rick," Emily says. "Go."

Kevin starts walking towards the transport and Rick follows. "Do you know anything about the XLM?" Rick asks.

"My father helped make the metal stronger and lighter," Kevin says.

Kristof is holding his helmet in his mechanized hand and as he enters the hatchway of the transport, his arm unnaturally swivels and the helmet avoids the side of the vehicle.

"What's the stuff he's wearing?" Rick asks.

"I have no idea," Kevin says. "Armor."

"His arm doesn't move right," Rick says.

"It's robotic. It's a machine," Kevin says.

Their feet do not echo on the interior fabric of the XLM and they sit while Kristof closes the hatchway behind them closing off their view of the others.

CHAPTER 14

The Armored Caste intended for the XLM to be easily manufactured and capable of transporting either civilians or fighters for the Empire. The goal was an easily assembled vehicle with a bare set of amenities, cushioning over hard benches, and no other comfort of note. It was a solid vehicle, which was the only good thing that could be said of it.

Kristof sat at the front console and looked back at the teenagers as his right arm worked a lever between the wall and seat. He was not wearing his helmet.

"What's your plan, guys?" Kristof asks.

Rick says, "I want to go back to Militia Wing."

"Alright," Kristof says and he turns towards the front again.

"Is that where you're taking us?" Rick asks.

"No," Kristof replies. "Not now," he says after a minute. "Why do you want to go back to Militia Wing?"

Rick starts to speak and then stops. Kevin realizes Rick is angry and tired and he's tired too, but he tries to keep the Vision Caste in his thoughts while listening to their conversation. The Vision Caste released several screens regarding the Anarchists not long ago, as well as a few of the outside world. Right now he wasn't sure which to believe, his eyes or the screens.

Rick begins to grow tired but soon picks his head up again. "Take us back to Militia Wing." Playing in Rick's mind and the edge of his vision are shades of colors and pales of clouds, dark and stormy, lightning and criss-crossed, there is no end or depth as he tries to bring his mind to some semblance of an understanding. There is nothing to grasp, there is nothing he can do.

He can simply believe what he is seeing is happening if he wishes to, and this is asked of him somewhere in this space he is in.

There is nowhere to run, there is nowhere to go, he is told there.

He didn't ask for where he was, inside of his mind or out, but there was an idea or a change or a semblance that somehow something in someway had gone terribly wrong, because of the sorrow he felt, and the hurt, even if he denied what he was dealing with.

He did not know what was happening and he was tired. There was no talk beforehand, there were no explanations for why he was where he was. There was no preparation for events such as these, yet he was given the means to live and do so by the very fact that anything at all was placed in front of him, whether he wanted it or not, or whether it even existed or not, in his dream, or in the world, in his mind or outside of it, and ultimately whether he believed anything made sense or did not.

He only clung to what he knew and eventually understood he held on to something and did not know where it came from.

"We're almost there," Kristof says.

Kevin looks out the window and watches again as the trees pass by. Kevin decides he would join Jake if he could, fight for the Vision Caste, and do what he could to end the wars that had brought the attack to his city.

Kristof was already aware of this.

"Don't bother, Kevin," Kristof says. "You won't get anywhere with that."

"What?" Kevin asks because he hadn't spoken.

"The plant, gaze, did Aaron tell you about it?"

"A little, yes," Kevin says. "It's a plant?"

"I can see your mind," Kristof says.

Kevin's eyes widen and then he suddenly blinks back tears of fright.

"Do you know where you will be tomorrow, Kevin?"

Kristof asks.

"No?"

"Neither do I," says Kristof.

"Then what's going on? What are we doing?"

"The wars are about to start, Kevin. Well, they will soon."

"What do you mean?" Kevin asks.

"There won't be enough gaze any longer."

"What is gaze? What is it really?" Kevin asks.

"It's a plant from cities like the one you are from," Kristof says.

Kevin folds his hands. "I thought the wars have been going on for years?"

Kristof is quiet for a moment. "The cities aren't able to make gaze for enough people. The real wars are about to start."

"I thought you can't die?" Kevin asks.

"No, I can die." He pauses a moment. "So will a lot of people. It's going to get very bad."

"What do you mean?" Kevin asks, upset.

"You'll see," Kristof says. "There are many that will not understand what is happening or why."

"What do you mean people are going to die?" Kevin asks him.

"Gaze allows you to see other's minds and it heals your body when you eat it," Kristof explains. Giving Kevin a hard look, he pauses again, deciding how much to share before continuing. "You eat it, or you die."

Kevin notices the trees have vanished and the transport is traveling smoothly through high grass. "You have to eat it?"

"Yes, if you do, you will always need it."

"There's not enough?" Kevin asks.

"One of the cities in South America is responsible for larger amounts of gaze, but they won't be making any more."

"Empire City?" Kevin asks.

"I don't know," Kristof turns the wheel in front of him and pulls down another handle on the console and the XLM comes to a firm stop and settles back slightly. He presses a button and the vehicle lowers. Rick is jostled out of his sleep.

The door is pulled back on the side of the vehicle and

Kevin, Rick and Kristof stand out in the open air and the sun is setting.

"Is there water?" Rick asks. They are hurt, scared and lonely, but comforted by the fact they know each other from Militia Wing. The vehicle, with Emily, Rick, and Jake, is heard pulling up as Kristof is undoing the clasps of his breastplate.

"This way," he says. Kevin follows Kristof and Rick waits for the vehicle to come to a stop.

Aaron hops out of the vehicle and grins at Rick, "I think your friend Jake is doing better."

"Can you get him some water, Aaron?" Emily asks.

"Sure." He begins looking through a part of the wall of the building that had fallen away. He heads towards the run-down and decaying structure and Rick follows him. There is a subtle shift in the tension between the two.

Emily leans down and wipes the sweat from Jake's forehead. His color was still pale and slightly sick, but he had stopped shivering. The sweat glistened on his face and forehead and his upper lip curled slightly, reminiscent of the slight half-smile she had come to know from him.

"Jake," she whispers and wipes his forehead again.

He stirs a little at the sound of her voice. "They were going to kill us."

"I know, Jake," she says and touches his hair.

"We have to stop them," he says.

"I know," she says and her eyes tear as she looks away from him.

"No one believes me," Jake says and his eyelids flutter.

"I know, Jake," Emily says again and tears spill down her cheeks.

Behind a locked door, Kristof unrolls a length of fabric from the ceiling and attaches a wire from each corner to separate plug-housings resting in the floor. A thick and protected metal cable runs from each housing to a large generator. After making sure the plugs are situated, Kristof stands in front of the generator and makes some adjustments. The fabric diffuses ethereally in the air in front of them, like blue mist.

A few faces appear. Kristof looks at the others seated around the room, "Get up," he says to Rick and Kevin. "You can use your hands to adjust the figures," he says.

"When can we sleep?" Kevin asks.

"Soon," Kristof says. His eyes are glassy and shining with a far-off obsession as he uses his normal hand to turn the faces of the men who have appeared in front of them this way and that.

Aaron rises off of a haphazardly balanced wooden chair and diplomatically looks around the room. "Kristof, I need to get back to Rio soon, maybe we should figure out what is going to happen with these kids?"

Kristof stops adjusting the figures and looks back at the others, his eyes still shining with the light of a man who had not heard of salvation, but had seen it.

"I want two of them," Kristof says, looking at Aaron.

"Excuse me?" Aaron says.

He drags his good hand across his beard. "I want two of them to stay behind," he says. "I don't care which of them stay. You can take the girl back."

Jake was lying in a cot and slowly turned over to lie on his side.

"You're going to help us, right?" Jake says weakly.

Kristof's focuses on Jake and his eyes narrow. "Yes, of course, I'm going to help you."

"I'll stay," Jake says after a moment.

Kevin speaks up before Rick has a chance to say he was going to stay with Emily, "I'll stay here, too."

The room is dark and musty, the wood is old and rotted in some places. There is only a dim light in the room from outside and the illumination of the fabric.

Kristof sits back in an old chair in the corner of the room. In the darkness, he grips the arms of the chair and his head imperceptibly rocks back and forth.

"You want to turn this thing off?" Aaron asks from the center of the room.

"No," Kristof says. "I can't get you a map to Rio," He sniffs loudly. "I'm not connected to anything out here. I only have what I can secure myself."

"That's fine, I know how to get back to Rio, Kristof." He looks at the others. "Why don't we sleep? Talk about this afterward?" He ducks his head and looks out through a vacant part of a wall that could have been a window, and night was growing. "It's probably what, 6, 7? If we sleep now, we can leave before the sun rises."

Kristof looks down at his mechanical arm and the hand rotates in a circle. "I prefer noon, myself," he says.

Aaron steps cautiously towards Kristof, "That's fine, Kristof. Noon is a perfect time to have a nap, that's what my mother always said." He grins and the lines on his face betray his casualness. He habitually wipes his hand across his smile. While he is thinking of something to say, Kristof interrupts his seeming ease.

"Is your mother alive, Aaron? When was the last time you saw your mother?" he asks, quietly.

Aaron's eyebrows flutter and his eyes turn dark.

"I'll let the children sleep, but they will get up before sunrise. There is a makeshift water shower behind the building. I'll use the generator to heat it," Kristof states.

Aaron looks at Kristof darkly and Kevin realizes there is more to this conversation than what is being said.

"The clothing?" Aaron asks.

"Wash them in the shower, I'll dry them," Kristof replies.

"I can't take anyone to Rio in those clothes," Aaron states.

Kevin looks down at his clothes, his light grey jacket is torn and his threaded shirt is stained. Aaron was wearing a long cloak and his shirt underneath was ruffled around the neck, with bright colors that made Kevin's and the clothes of the others look drab and dull by comparison. It was the type of clothing worn only by the wealthy in the domes.

"I don't care what you can or can't do," Kristof was saying. "The two boys staying with me do not need any other clothing than what they are wearing. They will learn to care for them."

Kevin gripped his bag. One of his shirts was stained with Jake's blood and he only had two others. He did not know if Jake was prepared, but they were roughly the same size. Kevin suddenly thought of his mother and involuntarily let out a choking sob.

"Oh, why--," Emily begins, and she starts crying quietly.

A spell is broken over the room, the breaking point had been reached for the group as the full weight of what was happening settled down on them. Their lives were irrevocably changing, and not with their full cooperation or understanding.

Rick stiffens in his chair and Kevin could see that he was trying to adopt the rigid posture that Aaron affected and he seemed to not notice Emily was crying.

Kevin reached over to her and tried to smile.

"I don't understand," she says and she sobs, more quietly then she had.

"This old coot is saying that there are more cots in another room," Aaron says. "Let's get them set up."

CHAPTER 15

I Each day I write in this note, a little each day, to remind the children that not one of us has a choice in the way things are. Each day they bring the wood to me and we build a fire so we will remember the old ways.

They were not disciplined before I met them. On the first day, I swiftly struck the loud one about the head with a piece of wood I required of him. I spoke to him and said to bring more like it. The quiet one had taken a fierce stance but I quelled it with another stick to the head and it was done.

They slept the better part of the day. I told them they were free to leave. I explained to them they could go at any time, but they have nowhere to go as I have nowhere to go, and I can see their minds.

They have left off with these foolish notions of rebellion and they fetch the wood and I reward them with rations I have sequestered from the packs of dead men. It pains me to even write any more on the subject, so I tell them and so it is, and they have learned.

I strike them daily, as is my character, and is the character of the old ways. I am preparing them for the war that is coming, the war I can sense. We have no lack of food and I find gaze here and there, and I still receive my rations every second full moon from the men at the Great Lakes.

I have a green pass, an old pass, and they know they are to hand me gaze without question, but I can see of the men that it is no longer so freely given, and we speak little, and I say even less, and I leave.

The boys have asked to come with me on my outings a time or two. I have put an end to such foolish nonsense that even the loud one will barely say a word during supper and it is quiet and it is pleasant. I think tomorrow they will be ready to learn to handle unarmed weapons and I will never let them near anything else.

For you,
Kristof

Jake and Kevin pulled their covers around themselves tighter and listened to some of the boards creak in the ramshackle building as a strong wind blew through.

They were happy to find that the man, Kristof, slept, though he would not sleep at regular hours. Sometimes he woke up at night and would drag them out of bed, but other nights he would fall fast asleep.

Tonight they were afraid, as they usually were, but there is a type of peace that only comes in the midst of terror and it had found a place to dwell inside them, as they listened to the man snore in the other room.

Jake had more trouble than Kevin when it came to nights like this. Jake would be unable to sleep when the man snored, and they both had gotten so used to the dark circles under each other's eyes they didn't notice them any longer.

"He's crazy, Kevin."

"I know," Kevin said.

It had been some time since Rick and Emily had left with Aaron. Not so long between their departure and the previous life which had been so shattered. It was almost a dream from another lifetime, and all his fears and expectations of those times were so small in comparison.

The wind would often blow through holes in the moldy building they slept in and the large insects Kristof called 'grasshoppers' were not afraid to jump or crawl on anything.

Jake shivered and tried to pull the threadbare covering over his head.

"How are we going to leave, Jake?" Kevin said.

"I don't know," Jake replied.

They had given up wondering if the man Aaron would come back, with or without Emily or Rick. Jake assumed that, eventually, he would, but Kevin was not so sure.

"He didn't even know Kristof before he met him, Jake!" Kevin said, but Jake had a reserve of hope in the future that refused to be diminished and was probably the reason why Jake had been so popular in school.

"You never know, Kevin," he had said. "He might still come back."

This was part of an endless conversation the two had while huddled on their cots. Tonight, the conversation focused on another topic which was gaining more appeal with each passing day.

"We can still try to follow the road back home," Jake was saying. They did not use the words 'Militia Wing' any longer. 'Home' had become the world that was left behind.

"Yeah," Kevin said. He closed his eyes and tried to sleep while the loud droning of the insects inside the building did everything they could to remind him of where he was.

"Tyler? Tyler, is that you?" A woman's voice from further in the apartment called out. Aaron put a finger to his lips and ushered the two teenagers in through the door.

"Yes, Melissa, it's Tyler!" Aaron called out.

A young woman with dark hair peeked her head around the corner. "Aaron?" she said, surprised.

"The one and only!" His face breaking out in a broad grin.

The young woman smiled and Emily could see she was wearing an intricately designed floral apron she wiped her hands on the front of, before turning back around the corner.

"Come in, Aaron! Sit down! I'm almost done here."

The apartment was bright and sunny and the smell of baking pastries filled the air. The ceilings were much higher than any of the ones in the Militia Wing dorms and the apartment was on the second floor of a large building with many stories. Aaron had led the two teenagers through a maze of hallways and a staircase or two, and Rick and Emily had quickly become disoriented and were not sure they could find their way out.

"The place is as lovely as ever," Aaron replied and sat down on a fabric covered couch near the front door. "Have a seat," he said quietly to the teenagers. He had already explained to them not to say very much and to tell anyone who asked that they were from a city in the Great Lakes area.

Rick had argued about this until Emily calmed him down and he finally understood there wasn't much they could do on their own to get back, or if there was anything left at all.

Inside Emily was a hidden and changing pillar of thought and feelings she could easily conceal. Rick envied her ability to hide behind a calm face, his thoughts and feelings were always so plain for anyone to see. Biting his lip, he tried to emulate Emily and seem at ease.

"Just be calm, act casual," Aaron whispered to the two. Emily explained to Rick during their journey here, that 'teenagers' simply meant anyone that was school-aged.

"Who do you have with you?" The woman asked from the other room.

Aaron ducked his head. "Ah, they're two kids I met from that job I had up in the Great Lakes."

"Ah," was the reply.

Rick looked around the living space. Bright, cheerful colored lights were shining from the ceiling and upper walls that slowly moved and changed over time. He looked around to see if he could find the source of the lights. The couches and loveseat were a pale cream color and the walls were a light sky blue, with a thick and gauzy red carpeting with more interesting patterns. A black sharp-angled table rested near where the two teenagers sat.

Melissa came down the hallway holding a white tray with several pastries and a cloth underneath.

"This is the first batch. I just put the last of it in the toaster," she says, placing the tray and cloth down on the low table. She eyed the two teenagers with an arched eyebrow, her dark hair was pulled back into a ponytail, and the low cut shirt she wore revealed much of her neck and chest.

Emily was looking at Rick and Rick's face suddenly grew red. Aaron broke out into another grin.

"Try not to touch them right away," Melissa said. "They're hot." She turned and went back to the kitchen.

After she had left, Aaron gave the two a thumb's up and silently mouthed a few words.

"How long are you staying this time?" Melissa asked from the kitchen.

"Ah, not long," Aaron said.

"You are such a mudder," Emily said to Rick. She grabbed one of the pastries and fanned it with her hand. The two men quickly looked at Emily aghast and her face tensed and she swallowed involuntarily. She then noticed that Rick was staring more at the pastry. Aaron was looking at her with daggers and she cleared her throat. She sat back and began to eat the pastry.

"It's good," Emily said loudly. Aaron's face became white.

"Thank you, hun," was the reply from the kitchen. "Why don't you turn on the broadcast, Aaron?"

"Alright," Light and pale colors began to form and focus above the center of the room.

"I don't know what kind of broadcasters you've got up in the Great Lakes. I'm sure Aaron knows more about that than I do, but this one was the best I could afford," Melissa said from the kitchen.

The teenagers had not seen technology like this before. The closest anyone had in the dorms were the screens, unless you plugged directly in, but you needed an implant for that. The cloud of colors began to take shape and a panorama of tall buildings with a stage in the middle and a crowd of people standing on it could be seen. Rick blinked and rubbed his eyes.

"Here, take this, I'm going to go talk to Melissa," Aaron said and rose off the couch. He threw a small box to Rick. As he passed by he leaned down and whispered, "Don't press any of the buttons. You can turn that dial in the middle to rotate the view if you like." He straightened up and went down the hallway toward the kitchen area.

Rick began to turn the dial on the device and the scene rotated. He noticed it stayed fixed on the center of the stage. When he started to stand up to look closer, Emily put a hand on his arm.

"Just sit still, be quiet right now," Emily said.

Rick squinted his eyes and noticed a large part in the middle of the stage seemed to be missing. The view rotated around in a way that played tricks in his mind. A tall woman was standing near the missing spot, addressing the crowd, surrounded by several men and women who stood facing the crowd as well. The clouds in the sky above the scene stretched and blurred as the panoramic scene curved, but it went largely unnoticed since both teenagers were not very familiar with the way clouds acted, living under a dome their entire life up until now.

"Oh, you can't hear anything. I'm sorry!" the teenagers heard from within the kitchen. Soon it seemed the voice of the tall woman came from the walls around them.

"... due to the unfortunate collapse of several key structures within Empire City," the woman was stating.

A larger man to her right spoke up and Rick and Emily realized he was addressing the woman and not the crowd.

"You had no plan during the construction regarding earthquakes? Seismic activity?" he asked, addressing her, even if his words were for the audience. He wore a top hat with an electronic band above the brim that contained shifting colors. He was a portly man and his shirt fit snugly over his massive stomach, the buttons stood out prominently and shined as gold in the sun.

"The parts of the city that fell to the earthquake were constructed several hundred years ago. Renovations had been scheduled," the woman replied.

Another man spoke up, a tall thin man, pale white with long blonde hair. "And this was the same earthquake that caused the damage to Militia Wing, only so close to us here in dear Rio, ma'dam?"

"Yes, as I have already stated. We believe an abandoned transit tunnel collapsed and this corroborates with the evidence of the structures that fell," she said.

The thin man paused, rubbing his lips with a finger, looking off into the distance as if he were barely listening to her. As if she herself were simply a matter of consequence in a larger story and the words she used were mere toys in a larger game. He grinned.

"So this is why we felt nothing of any earthquake in Rio?" he stated.

"Yes, Mr. Brennar, and let me remind you we are broadcasting across the Empire, we are not only concerned with Rio and what happens here," and she planted her feet firmly. The same thin man, Brenner, waved his hand idly, then paused again to look at the woman with a solemn grace and silently nodded.

The portly man, who had not been named, spreading his large arms, exposing his barrel chest and gut behind his thick gold buttons to all around, said, "Then to what do we owe this gracious visit, Sen Lucinda? The city of Rio greatly appreciates the Empire's concern and care for its citizens, and we would like to assure the Empire that had I, and I'm sure Mr. Brenner and Sen Kendall, been in the area during its construction, we would be cursing ourselves, as well, for our own oversight and the loss of so many lives."

Rick swiveled the picture and the crowd was looking at the large man with beaming eyes at this statement. He noticed several hands were raised in the air and scattered cheers among the crowd.

"Of course, Mr. Steinem. As are we--"

The picture moved forcefully towards the floor of the platform the group was on, and nothing could be seen but dirt and metal. Emily looked at Rick sharply.

"Sorry, it's this dial," Rick said.

"-- we believe the construction of the Avena Tower should begin again," the woman said.

"Here in our great city?" Steinem exclaimed.

"Yes. We believe it will help in the Empire's mission if we finish construction of a tower so close to 'Militia Wing'."

"That will bring great fortune to our fair Rio!" Steinem finished and closed his hands in fists. The thin man, Brenner, muttered behind his hand and seemed lost in thought. The third man stood quietly from his seat.

"Who will begin construction?" the third man said evenly.

The woman paused and looked to Steinem and Brenner for help. Finally, she addressed the third man, Sen Kendall, and Rick believed he heard a tremor in her voice.

"We are looking at your local businesses," she stated.

Applaud and cheers came from the crowd and Steinem raised his hands and grinned. Brenner curtly nodded. Kendall seemed lost in thought.

"What about the attack?" Rick whispered and he looked at Emily.

"They're not mentioning the attack on our city at all," Emily said.

Aaron came up the hallway and the subtle scent of his hot drink wafted into the room. He sipped the drink and addressed the teenagers. "How are you two getting along?"

"These people aren't talking about the attack on our city!" Rick said.

Aaron choked and looked back down the hallway towards the kitchen. "Cool it, okay? As far as anyone needs to know, you two are from a place called West Springs in the Great Lakes area and that is all that anyone needs to know." He recovered his composure and gazed at the picture in the room.

"Also, you're not going to hear anything about it either. I'm betting that, according to the Empire, the attack never happened. Please keep quiet about any of it, okay? Here, let me see the pinger," he says, reaching his hand out.

Rick looked at Aaron absently and Aaron moved his hand again. Emily hit Rick in the arm and pointed at the device in his hands.

"Here," Rick said.

Aaron adjusted the picture and the clouds came into focus. The lines on the men and women became sharper and more defined. "You guys are all used to that newer stuff up there in West Springs, it's all automatic," he said loudly.

Aaron leaned down and whispered. "West Springs is not a real place, but it's a close enough job for having no time. I explained to Melissa that you two went to a special school. There's--"

He quickly stopped and stood up as Melissa came down the hallway.

"So, they're starting work on the Avena Tower again?" she said to Aaron and leaned against the wall, wiping her hands with a cloth.

"Avena?" Aaron said.

"You've turned white, Aaron!" Melissa said and laughed as she playfully hit Aaron in the chest. "Tell me you're not superstitious, too!"

"No, I--" Aaron started to say.

"How long have I known you, Aaron?" Melissa asked him.

He took a sip of his coffee. "A few years, off and on."

"Right, you've spent all this time in Rio and you're still superstitious about Avena! You really are a country bumpkin," she said teasingly and smiled.

"Well, I just-- I didn't know."

"What do you guys think out there in the sticks? I've heard such wild stories," she said. Aaron looked back and Rick was looking at him angrily.

Get it together, Aaron thought. Even this kid sees right through you.

A crashing thunderstorm had settled above the abandoned building Kristof called home and the waves of rain riding on the wind slid in through the cracks in the cement and the cracks in the boards. Looking around, a feeling crept up Jake's spine that this man Kristof had lived here for far too long. It was an unnatural feeling, a primitive feeling, and Jake realized he'd been fooled. This man did not belong where he was, nor would he ever help them with anything at all.

There was no talk about the Anarchists, or returning home, or Avena, or any of it. He huddled in his chair tighter, pulling his ragged blanket around his shoulders and tried to ignore the guilt he felt for the loss of Kevin's family. He couldn't look Kevin in the eyes, and his anger with Kristof bled into an anger with life itself, only to dissipate and funnel back into his own mind. He had retracted and retreated from the events around him and his eyes had grown hollow and despondent.

"We have to tell Kristof about what we saw," Kevin was saying.

A spark rose in Jake's mind and Kevin thought he saw a flicker of Jake's old, arrogant self across his face.

"I don't know what good it will do," Jake said. "We don't know what it was, and..." Jake paused. "He won't understand it and he'll use it against us."

Kevin had noticed Jake had taken Kristof's actions personally, he had taken what the man said and did as his own personal responsibility.

Initially, Jake had been the strong one, the champion of the cause, although they had no idea what cause bound them together, other than circumstance and shared history. Those days were forcing Kevin to become the stronger of the two.

"Maybe it will change him and change what's happening," Kevin said.

Somehow, Kevin noticed Kristof had become focused on Jake, moving with a wariness around him, although Kevin found this train of thought confusing. Kristof's voice would rise to a higher pitch when speaking to Jake, though he would never address him directly or even look him in the eye. Kevin wondered if the scrutiny between the two allowed Kevin to see events for what they were and allowed him to gain some type of hope.

Kristof told the two he was leaving for several days. He made no mention of food or survival or care and had left. It was obvious to Kevin that Kristof did not care what happened to the two of them.

Kristof did not seem to eat much, however, occasionally he would force the two to sit with him while eating. Kevin had checked some of the cupboards and other rooms in the building and had found various packs of food lying around, though attempts had been haphazardly made to hide them.

The day before, Kevin and Jake noticed a large aerial craft in the distance. Kevin was more familiar with Armored Wing vehicles and did not recognize the vehicle at all, though he knew Armored Wing manufactured several types of aerial crafts and they initially assumed it to be with Armored Wing.

Jake had become excited, pointing the vehicle out to Kevin, hoping the vehicle would notice them.

It did not fly directly in the direction of the building, but it flew close enough that Kevin and Jake could identify what seemed to be an image on the side of the vehicle, and it was not related to anything the two had seen from Armored Wing at all. The material covering the outside of the aerial craft appeared slightly translucent as the light from the sun seemed to shimmer around and through it. On its side was a large black area that appeared to be part of the vehicle itself, and on this black area was a red half-circle.

Noticing this, the two hid in the trees, knowing if the vehicle was searching for signs of life, they were found.

The next morning Jake noticed what he thought was one of the local animals inside of the abandoned building. On closer inspection, he realized it was mechanical. It was an automaton fitted with sensors. He ran in fear to find Kevin but it was gone when they both returned.

"Someone will be here soon, someone will find us," Kevin had said.

Jake blinked his eyes several times and his eyebrows furrowed. "Then, don't tell Kristof," he remarked. "It'll be a surprise."

He looked at Kevin for the first time in several days.

"Please," he said quietly. "Don't tell him anything."

Kevin tried to blink back tears.

"Okay, Jake," he said.

CHAPTER 16

The The loose wooden door was violently kicked in and from an empty space in the wall that had once held a window, a large metal object flew in and landed on the ground. A high pitched whine came from the device and a blinding light that seemed almost purple flashed suddenly.

Kristof had ducked under a nearby table and covered his head in time to avoid the blue-white light. Kevin, turning towards the crashing door, was blinded almost immediately. He fell to his knees, trying to shield his eyes from further damage, unable to see the approaching men.

"Tell us where your gaze is," a deep and loud synthetic voice crackled through the settling noise.

Kevin stopped moving as a boot shoved down on his back, firmly holding him to the ground. "Cover your ears, kid," he heard a voice above him yell loudly from a few feet above.

Kevin barely had time to cover his ears with his hands when a burst of sound ran through his body from the device on the floor, releasing a shockwave that blew apart Kristof's eardrums and rendered Kevin faintly deaf.

"Tell us where your gaze is," the synthetic voice stated again, though to Kevin's mind the words were muffled and far away, fumbling through layers of cotton. Kevin was hauled upwards, opening his eyes, his vision was still flashing. He closed them tightly shut and panicked.

He vaguely heard a muffled destructive sound and he

realized he could faintly smell Jake. It was the best he could understand of his situation before he was pulled violently backward and something was placed against the back of his head and then everything was gone.

The man dragged Kevin's listless body out of the building, pushing forward as the 'bio-damper' flashed a blinding light again and did its work. He laid Kevin's body in the grass and pulled his legs and arms out from under him and tucked them to his sides.

The other boy was unceremoniously thrown to the ground, and Maxy went over to the body and repeated the same action. He knew someone who had once been hit with one of these guns and had woken with a bone out of its socket. Maxy did not believe it necessary to put prisoners through more pain then necessary, but none of the others shared his philosophy, so he simply did what he could when he could. He could not stop the others from causing it to happen, nor convince them of any real need to exercise caution, and was not quite sure he understood his own reasoning, aside from having been asked to avoid the unnecessary pain, so he did.

The device inside the building had three stages on a timer. One was an auditory message, one was a blinding flash of light, and one was a deafening shockwave. Several of the men were wearing helmets to protect their eyes and ears.

The only weapons he carried were the knockout gun which worked at point-blank range and a pistol. Only three people had been scouted in the area, so he placed the knockout gun on the ground and aimed his pistol at the door with both hands.

The chatter of the other men was heard through the pickup in his helmet. The man left inside had taken gaze and the others were having trouble subduing him. Maxy hated gaze and found it only slightly ironic that his job was to find and take it. It wasn't burned, disposed of or destroyed, it was given to his employer, so there was no satisfaction in his work at all.

Maxy holstered his pistol and pressed two separate buttons embedded in his wrist. In his mind's eye, from an implant inserted into his brain, he was able to see the visual pick up of the various men in the building just in time to see the face of the man on gaze in front of him as it blew apart from a powerful gun blast to the skull.

He stood outside the building and pressed the buttons in his wrist again to turn the images off.

"Come closer," the voice said.

Kevin tried to still the tremble in his legs as he walked down the wide corridor. The carpet that led to a pedestal at the end of the hall was a deep, dark red, with a simple pale gold line on each side, running the length of it.

Walking towards the voice, the pedestal moved farther away. Fearful, he stopped.

"That is not what I asked you to do, Kevin. Come closer," the voice urged again.

Squinting his eyes, he could vaguely make out a dark shape behind a desk on the marble pedestal. Pulling together the image, he realized the pedestal was simply smaller circles of marble on top of each other, each one smaller than the one below it, creating steps to the figure behind the desk. On the walls to the right and left, long dark tapestries hung, black with a red half-circle.

"Closer!" the voice yelled, even as he moved farther away, before the echoes of his command even had a chance to fade away. Kevin fell to his knees.

"Good," the voice said from behind him, and Kevin felt fingers slowly grip his shoulder. He turned suddenly and a shape of a man flickered in and out of his vision, blurred and moved quickly around him.

Kevin found himself walking aside the blurred figure. The man wore a high collared shirt and extravagant coat with a cape billowing behind him.

"Do you even know what pains I have taken to begin to understand an inkling of truth, Kevin?" the figure asked.

Kevin looked down at himself, it seemed as if he was invisible. He had no control of his actions, and no body to take any action with.

"I am a scholar," the figure said. It waved an arm towards

the desk and tapestries behind the empty pedestal.

"This is mine, this is my work," disappearing with the last word from Kevin's sight.

Kevin found himself immersed in liquid behind glass, and the figure was on the other side of the glass, waving.

"Who are you?" Kevin tried to say, but could not.

"I am Rutgers," the man said, in Kevin's mind. The figure stood still and simply waited, arms behind his back.

"What is this?" Kevin asked again, though he could not speak.

"This is my work, Kevin," the man said from behind the glass. "Well, this is the work of one of my staff."

"Why am I here?" Kevin said again, to anyone. To the figure, to the other person who had been indicated, to anyone that could hear, anywhere.

"Our tests show you were born in one of the Empire's plantations that is nearby. You are loyal to what you have learned within and I am simply making an attempt to appeal to your reason," the figure said.

Kevin found a sense of mental balance at the mention of 'plantation' and decided he would remain quiet for the time being.

"You see, Kevin, this is a test of my own conviction, I have thought about it for several days since you were brought to me. I have decided I would be completely honest with you and see if I could convince you of the merit of my own philosophy."

"It appears to me that you are the perfect subject for this. Do not fear, because you will die in either event. Do not believe you can say anything I wish to hear, you can not save your own life with your words, whether you agree with me or not. I will end your life when this is done, in either way, and I will be satisfied that I have proven my own reasoning to be the correct one," the figure stated.

Kevin thought of the word 'loyalty' the figure used, and the mention of a member of his staff, and wheels began turning in his mind.

"This is a simulated experience, Kevin, and it is also your last. You will not see anything beyond this, you have already left the world as you know it. Your body is 'lying on a table, hooked to a machine' as it were, but rest assured, these will be the last of your experiences. You may as well entertain my notions before you die. I believe, so far, you can agree with the merits of my notions?" the figure stated.

Kevin became alarmed and nodded quickly.

"Good, I see you have a sense of humor," the figure stated. "You agree with me, I would not be so quick to end your life," the figure said. "I am not finished. We will take our time, this is of benefit to you, isn't it?" and it seemed to Kevin that the figure behind the glass nodded as if agreeing with and assured of its own good sense.

"Yes," Kevin said, more boldly.

"Good," the man, Rutgers, said.

Kevin's last memory came to him of being blinded and deafened.

Some time passed and Rutgers spoke. "I will start, then, as it seems you will not."

"I am amassing an army. I am a student of history. I have access to knowledge I am assured that no one alive today has access to," Rutgers said.

"An army for what?" Kevin asked after some time.

Rutger looked off into the distance. "I am amassing an army to protect the citizens of the world who need protection," he said simply.

"Protection from what?" Kevin asked, striving for time and some type of balance.

"Death."

"Doesn't an army kill people?" Kevin asked. "Doesn't an army cause death?"

"It does, Kevin. I am already aware my philosophy is flawed, as are any and all that I have found to study. As are any and all men I have been able to find. This is why I need strength. I believe some ideas, some thoughts, some actions, and some philosophies are stronger than others. I believe strength comes from conviction, clear-sightedness, and sober-mindedness. I believe an enemy with less conviction, less sight, unable to reason clearly, will lose. I believe the flaws in men have given rise to the need for power."

"I believe conviction and strength comes from solid reasoning and emotional resolution. I grew up in a different world from the one we are in now, and so I know the world we live in today is merely an orchestration of events by various powers that be, to subdue the past and hide the truth to ensure the prevailing vision."

Kevin's mind was taken to the Vision Caste.

"Do you know about the Vision Caste?" Kevin asked.

"I do," Rutgers said simply.

"Do you know about Avena?" Kevin asked.

"I do, though I am aware there is no such place. The world was very different only a few hundred years ago. The people who are alive today have been led to believe that things have always been the way they are now. I am aware they have not been this way at all. I am aware it was the introduction of gaze into the population that caused this to change, for one."

"What is gaze?" Kevin asked. Somewhere in his mind, he had resigned himself to his fate and simply sought the answers to his questions before he would die. Such is the strength and innocence of youth.

"Gaze is a plant, Kevin. It grants a type of immortality. There is not enough gaze in the world for everyone, and this is why I am amassing an army."

"Where does it come from?" Kevin asked.

"That I do not know, and I hope to discover it. I do know 'Avena' was a recent idea, created to explain the effects of gaze to the population, without revealing gaze itself. There have been other attempts."

"Are you an Anarchist?" Kevin said.

"No. The Anarchists are people who are willfully trying to wrestle control of gaze from the Empire, the ones who built and control the plantations like the one you are from. The Empire is, or are, the only ones with the secret of gaze."

"What do you mean 'secret of gaze'?"

"No one is able to create it, though the Empire seems to be able."

"Doesn't that make you an Anarchist?" Kevin said loudly.

"That's not really a valid comparison. I do not profess to be one and my aims are different. The Anarchists tend to be comprised mostly of those who have defected from the Empire. But, I do make use of them, Kevin."

"Who are the Grippers then?"

"You can liken me more to the Grippers if you would like, though I do not claim to be a part of that group either. They are simply regular people from the population who have a direct need for gaze. They work closely with the Anarchists."

"It seems to me, from my research, the means to create it was discovered several hundred years ago. Soon after this, the Empire was founded, and then ultimately the plantations were started. It has always been my own private suspicion that even back then, men were confounded by the problem of having so many people alive on the Earth with no means to support them all."

"There have been several wars to change history for the people alive today, to hide why things are the way they are, or to change the way things are, or even to try and reveal something of truth, but it has not changed the nature of our existence."

"I seek simply to discover the means of gaze, and should my ambitions prove strong enough, implement a new and better way for those on Earth to survive. I understand that those who do not take gaze will live and die to their lives, and there is nothing that stops it. They are living in a world fabricated by those of us with the power of immortality, but to those who take it, we are at risk as our own population expands. There are further wars and divisions among us that there is not enough gaze for all, there never can or will be. Perhaps, most importantly, how do we control our own population, while dealing with more and more people who may either take it or not."

"There are over two billion people alive today, only a fraction take gaze, Kevin."

"Are you going to kill them all?"

"No," Rutgers said. "I am searching for a peaceful resolution. To do that, I must discover the means of creating gaze. I do not know if there is a solution to be found, but I also believe my solution is the best we may ever have for solving it."

"How am I supposed to believe you?" Kevin asked.

"What do you mean, Kevin?"

"I don't know how gaze works. I don't know if what you say is true. I have no way of giving you an answer."

Rutgers, in another part of the building, also hooked to the same simulation, paused and looked through the glass at Kevin. He realized, perhaps through the synthetic connections and habitations of each other's minds, the boy had resigned himself to die. The boy had experienced enough to know that he could not bring himself to blame or even grow angry at the inevitable.

In this moment of their two consciousnesses, they shared a bleak understanding of life. Some questions simply could not, or would not be answered. Should there ever be an answer, the question could never be.

They both found a peace. Time passed, and the echoes of their life force steadily rippled through the machinery.

"It's enough," Rutgers finally said, and his figure behind the glass shifted and flickered.

Kevin despaired as he realized he would lose his life. And should he not, he would see no reason to move forward, knowing nothing could be assured. He would always be at the mercy and fate of circumstances ultimately beyond any control.

"I could never understand," Kevin said bleakly to the man.

Rutgers paused and looked at the boy through the glass again.

"I can no longer leave this simulator, Kevin. To even try would destroy me, and the world may change by the time a solution was found."

"I provide power and services for many, however, with the abilities I have through this machinery. Having sacrificed my right to walk the Earth, I am aware enough to know there is still a hope for me in the future that I may be able to leave even this, someday."

"There are answers to questions and I know this now. We might not recognize them, we might not understand them, and maybe it is one of our flaws as human beings that peace may come from something other than what we seek, but I tell you, with truth, Kevin, the answers are there, somewhere."

Something changed in Kevin. A subtle shift in his own mind he could not understand.

"You will just kill me," Kevin said. "You got what you've wanted."

Rutgers, familiar with the mechanisms of the simulator, was aware something subtle had taken place. One thought crossed his mind and would not leave, if he ended the boy's life, it would mean nothing.

In his own fashion, he had proven himself to be right, and part of his conviction came from the change that takes place with resolution. He had sought the means to prove his own philosophy was the correct one. Strength was found in change and in growth through assurance.

He spoke with the boy, because he trusted the boy would die and so had sacrificed the boy's potential loyalty by using him to find proof of his own strength. He had reached a certainty that there was ultimately no right answer, only the strength of his position would see him prevail.

If he killed Kevin, it would prove his course of action was never changed by the knowledge he sought, because he would be taking the course of action he had intended to take from the outset, meaning he had learned nothing.

He would go on to solidify his forces and seek control of gaze and the means to produce it and convince others that his way was best, through force or persuasion. The assurance he had sought and gained in his conversation with Kevin was the strength of his own reasoning.

He looked at the young boy again, lying on a table somewhere, hooked to a machine that allowed him to be in his mind, and he to be in his, and the boy was waiting to die.

Rutgers realized that there was no response at all that would change his course of action.

"No," Rutgers said and knew what the boy would say before Rutgers ever said his next words. "You can live."

"So either you lied, your theory was wrong, or you used me for nothing,"

"No," Rutgers replied and took himself away from this

simulation into another one.

CHAPTER 17

"So you say, Toby," Menning said.

"I saw it today. I watched one," Toby said.

"A synthetic world, a synthetic world. Here? My stars, Toby, is it the stuff of nightmares?"

"Dreams and legends," Toby replied.

"Why would we do such a thing? It sounds like pure insanity."

"I don't understand it myself," and yet still, as Toby trailed his fingers lazily in the water, the light sail on the small boat moved them forward, rented for the afternoon.

He felt the need to express something he could not identify. Yet, it wasn't the desire to express something unbidden within himself that distracted him from the serenity of the clear, calm waters, the setting sun lending it's pink and red haze to the dark blue dusk. Instead, it was the feeling that anything needed to be unearthed within him at all, and this he found disconcerting. It did not take much reasoning to understand this type of ebbing feeling, on its own, could never be sated.

The feeling did not gnaw and puzzle hungrily at him, it was he that gnawed and puzzled hungrily at the feeling, he surmised.

"Is it a-- paradox?" Menning said haltingly, sitting beside Toby. "Is that what you said? A paradox-- you called it?"

"Something of the sort," Toby said distractedly.

Menning shivered. "Oh my stars, Toby, I can't even begin to imagine such a thing."

Toby pulled his fingers from the water and shook the water off.

"I feel this," he said. "I felt that!" he exclaimed.

"I know, I believe you," Menning said. He paused. "Toby, what's wrong with you?"

"I'm happy to be alive, that's all." Forlorn, he felt a little of the earth inside of himself breaking away.

"Why are you being so violent, Toby? What's gotten into you?" Menning said and his voice raised a pitch.

"Violent?" Toby responded.

"I don't like the way you're acting at all," Menning continued.

"Come on," Toby said. "Let's forget about it. We've got a little time before break hour, just enjoy this out here with me."

"Enjoy what? This?" Menning began bouncing on his knees in the small boat, sending ripples and currents along to the other passengers.

"Please stop," Toby said.

"What's wrong, Toby, none of these people out here like this. I only came out here because I have to. Do you think these other people feel any differently?"

Toby began to grow fearful. "What do you mean you have to?"

Menning sighed. "We've two choices, all of us. Before break hour we can come out here in the boats, or we can log in our rooms and read what's available. You're a scientist and you haven't figured that out, yet?"

"No?" Toby replied questioningly. Menning ignored him.

"Now, I like coming out here with you because you're different, Toby. You don't talk about the same things that a lot of the other people talk about, and dare I say, you talk with a kind of innocence I like and find refreshing. Which, honestly, I find almost impossible to believe given the position you have.

"Quite frankly, I'm almost shocked by the things you have already explained to me, and quite frankly, I keep my mouth shut about most of it, because for one, I don't think anyone would believe me if I told them, and for two, I don't think anyone could quite understand the things you talk about, because I sure as hell can't understand them most of the time. When I do think about them, I don't like where they lead, and I'd believe they were a product of, and I don't want to say your, but at least a deranged mind, if I did not already know that you were a part of the research lab, and had even seen you use your badge to enter that part of this establishment.

"However, let me inform you of something that maybe you might not quite like, or you might have a hard time dealing with, thinking about, or grasping. These people out here, do you see these people around you, around us, on this lake out here?"

"Yes," Toby replied hesitantly.

"They don't know or wouldn't even understand a thing you've been talking about, and it only leads me to believe that the rumors are true, the ones they come down on and cart away for spreading rumors, lies, dissension, the whole bit, are really the ones they end up giving all the power and control to behind closed doors, when it's all said and done, and quite frankly, you are proving it to me."

"But that's what I'm talking about!" Toby tried to reply without raising his voice. "None of this is real!" The surface of the water carried the hushed whisper far, however, and several other people from other boats turned their heads and looked quizzically at the pair.

Menning clenched his teeth and served Toby with an icy glare. "Toby," he responded quietly and with an effort to keep his tone, demeanor and posture pleasant, "Please lower your voice or you will have us both canned, if we are not headed there already." Menning felt dread and did his best to quell his fear so his visit with the bio-scanners would not reveal he had been exposed to any undue stress. He would be declared 'unfit' for his service, and possibly exposed to a life far worse than 'being canned'.

He had not even known the true reasoning behind the bio-scanners until he had met Toby who had begun, in his innocence and naivety, obliquely pumping Menning with dangerous information, simply in search of someone to bond with, share with, or possibly even call a friend.

On cue, almost, or at least as it seemed, Toby's demeanor

changed from a rare urgency to an almost soft and sickening pleading in which Menning was becoming accustomed.

"Please, Menning," Toby said.

"Explain it to me later," Menning stated.

"When?" Toby asked, still pleading, still angry, still hopeful. Still a little boy.

"At close hour. We'll meet at the rec rooms. Order a beer or two, but don't drink much of it. The cops know you eggheads don't like to drink much. They won't question it too deeply."

"Bring a friend," Toby said.

"What?" Menning said, and his shoulders suddenly slacked.

"Bring two or three if you can, as many as you can really, truthfully trust. Don't bring any more than that."

"What are you talking about, Toby?"

"Just do it, Menning."

"Are you here?" Tanya asked.

"I'm here," Kevin said from one of the tables in the room. He was hunched low.

"You can't get used to it, can you?" Tanya said, walking towards him.

Kevin waved his hand through a cup on the table. "No."

"It's okay, most everyone had a hard time adjusting."

Kevin looked over towards a table in the middle of the room.

Tanya followed his gaze. "Is that them?"

"Yep," Kevin said. "They're the ones that start it." After a moment, he asked, "Is it going to work this time?"

"Only one way to find out," she said.

The two walked closer to the table. Kevin doubled back. "You go first. I won't hear them yet."

Tanya paused. "Alright. Dutifully noted."

In all the spans, echoes and shapes of time, men either fall in one of two directions. They have foreknowledge, or they have insight, and all the times they get it wrong aside from the once or twice they get it right.

"Did we ever change a thing?" Kevin asked her.

"You aren't the first to say so," Tanya replied.

"Listen, Menning, I'm telling you, your name isn't Menning, it's something else! We're not actually here!" Kevin was close enough to finally hear one of them, Toby, at the table, stating.

"This is rubbish, Menning, why are we listening to this?" another man at the table, who would later be found out to be 'Alex Penning', if names had meant anything, and would also be found to be 'dead' in the oncoming discord that was about to take place.

"You've got three seconds, soon," Tanya said.

"Duly noted," Kevin smirked.

The luminescence that was indicative of Rutger's machinery hazily flickered and dimmed for a moment. Kevin was standing next to several guards who had slowly become interested in the developing spectacle at the table nearby.

Kevin, as he had done and tried several times before, and would always do again, waited for the second time the luminescence would dim.

As it did, he forcefully, and with purpose, smacked the automatic rifle out of the hands of one of the guards near to the table.

All hell broke loose.

CHAPTER 18

The walls around them began to stretch farther out and Menning found his face planted firmly inside the table.

"Liars, every single one of them is a liar."

Alex Penning's hand was inside the hand of another man at a nearby table.

"What was in this drink, Toby?" Menning yelled, and his voice carried far, far out into the wilderness of a scene he was staring down into, more alive and real than any other he had ever seen, as animals he couldn't even imagine sprinted and bounded underneath him through the landscape.

"It is a figment of your own imagination," a pleasant and soft female voice whispered to Toby.

The room suddenly snapped back to the way that it had been prior, and Toby and Menning watched with fearful dread as one of the men Menning had brought with him stood up from the table and pointed at the two.

"They just attacked the guard!"

The two, cow-eyed, turned and faced the rifles humming before them. The guards wore helmets that masked any trace of humanity, only their hands revealed their intent.

Toby, almost imperceptibly, noticed they stiffened, then a voice was heard from one of the men's helmets.

"You are under arrest. Remain still."

Toby and Menning had yet to move, though Menning was faintly registering shock.

"Isolation," the two heard. "Immobility." The two words came from the same speaker grille of the guard's helmet which had spoken earlier. Both words were intonated with an authorization register, a sound key used to determine the level of authorization an order was given in, and what level of security the authorization was handed down from.

An intonated order could only be addressed by the security level which had given it. The sound key used meant the security level was 'breach', meaning there was no authority that had given the order, which meant there was no authority who could address the order. None in the room had heard this particular sound register prior, as it was never meant to be heard.

Toby and Menning were unable to move. Their bodies still steadily beat with life, but their consciousness was reduced to perception and no more. They could not blink on their own if they tried. The two slowly slumped and fell quietly out of their chairs, and Menning found himself staring face first at the ground.

"It's not real, it's not real," Menning heard.

"Toby?" Menning thought.

"It's not real, it's not real," Menning heard in his mind, again, over and over.

"Toby, is that you?" Menning thought again.

It was Toby's voice. It was Toby's mind, Menning realized.

He was hearing Toby talking, or at least thinking, to himself.

"Toby, can you hear me?" Menning tried to think to him, as loudly as he could.

"It's not real, it's not real, it's not real," Toby was repeating to himself over and over again.

"What in Avena's sake is going on?"

"Tell us how you did it!"

"I'm telling you, I don't understand what happened!" Menning yelled.

"How did you break free?"

"What?" Menning answered incredulously.

And just like that, Menning DeFoster found himself naked, cold and shivering, lying on the damp, cold earth, around his ankle was a metal clamp, and inside the metal was some kind of tracking circuitry.

He groggily pushed himself up to his knees, wiped the dew from his slick shaved head, and took off running haphazardly into the open landscape. It took him several minutes before he realized his hands were bound together. He then realized they were not his own hands.

CHAPTER 19

Time passed. The Empire, with the support of the Vision Caste in the August Plantation, the last plantation built on Earth, was able to spread and support the idea that only certain members of the planet were granted an immortality due to their allegiance to mankind's homeworld, and not from a product manufactured in their plantations.

It had taken over a hundred years or so to reach the point to where this idea was believed and could affect some type of balance and help stabilize the population and explain their world.

The number of people who would never have access to gaze far exceeded the small handful who did. Originally, the people who needed gaze drafted other members of the world in powerful positions to slowly sway the tide of world events, enticing them with a free immortality on earth. In exchange, they were entitled to gaze. After several wars, with the key players unaware they were being guided and influenced by those with a knowledge and power of an increased lifespan, ability to heal, and a limited supply of a drug they could not do without.

Over time, the Empire was founded.

Eventually, mankind's descendancy from Avena had grown to become accepted by the majority of the population, and ascendency within was a matter of allegiance to the Empire and adherence to the rules set forth.

History had found an enemy, and it was born in mankind. Evidence of the past was destroyed, millions died over the centuries, and even the wars themselves and the causes of them were eventually concealed.

In a handful of generations, it was believed the chaos of the world was caused by mankind's struggle with Avena itself and the true people of Avena had retreated and left those on Earth to die or to get back on their own, if they could.

Others believed the state of the world was due to the struggle between the rising Vision Caste and the Anarchists, or even Avena itself and the Anarchists, and the Vision Caste continued to publicly decry all dissidents from the Empire under one label.

Cities were destroyed, leaving behind countless broken and failing technologies. Pockets of history could be found among the population, but they rarely corresponded with one another on why things were the way they were.

This was for the people who did not take gaze at all.

Some believed that the Earth itself did not exist, insisting mankind existed on Avena, and everything around them was a lie, an illusion. The power of those with immortality grew, large machines were constructed, weapons were made, palatial palaces built by slaves rose, and some secretly believed this was all being used to disguise the wars against the true leaders of Avena themselves.

The Grippers, though never publicly acknowledged by the Empire, remained as a collective hiding place for those with the knowledge of immortality. Inwardly defecting from the Empire's rule, they worked as double agents, sequestered supplies of gaze and created a black market, for any, beyond the ideals of the Empire or any subsequent group a person might be associated with. They worked in secret, the drug was of a limited supply, death came to any that could not have access to the drug at any given time.

The Empire's influence and power waned steadily as they continued to decry all opposed to the Empire as a group called the Anarchists, which steadily gained followers. A rebellious force opposed to the Empire's mission to restore peace with

Avena and eventually get mankind home to the safety of their homeworld. A mission, group and world history invented by the Vision Caste itself.

They labeled Earth a dangerous place and the Anarchists were simply a rebellious off-shoot of the human race, who wanted nothing more than to halt humanity's progress towards Avena, a peaceful civilization, freedom, and realization of its true meaning.

The world's history was slowly changing and being destroyed simply by those of the growing number who were alive long enough to affect it, and saw the need for change until they had the power to withstand the massive population who would never have the ability to access gaze.

Avena, being a civilization from another planet, a place watching mankind and attempting to guide it with means beyond the understanding of the population proved to be the most effective way of explaining any and all rationales and phenomena taking place on Earth, and the Empire affected this sovereignty strongly over the generations.

The idea had bite and it sunk in. Even those who had taken gaze for centuries began to believe the idea as their memories changed. Succumbing to their endless lifespan and ability to heal from any injury, they began to drastically alter their bodies as new technology allowed, making the possibilities for life on Earth limitless.

And then one day Rutgers, a man who had grown in power through years of gaze and powerful technological change and advancement, began the 'Plan of Indoctrination', which many members of civilization portrayed as a worldwide, massive execution.

He convinced other powerful members of the Empire that humanity, in and of itself, was useless. Their growing numbers did nothing more than sap the limited resources of the earth and endangered themselves with no rational governance or rule to guide them. If they could not be given an endless life, members of the population would be slated for 'preservation'. Their minds would be kept in an electronic and synthetic existence, their cell tissue sampled and collected, their bodies destroyed.

It was thought that many of those with no knowledge or access to gaze, born into a shattered world with no history or reasonable sense of why things were the way they were, with no power to implement change, would ultimately lie down to die.

"I'm nervous, Jake."

"Don't be, Emily, it's okay. We've been working out the technology. We've tested it multiple times, it's safe, you'll be okay," he replies.

"Are you sure?" she said.

"Yes. I can't see what you're doing, but it's easy enough to figure out. The kit I sent you only has a few dials and sensors, you'll get an idea of what to do."

Jake stood in a courtyard of the educational buildings Rutger's men were using to record as much information of citizens in the nearby areas they would need, in an attempt to preserve their names and lives.

It was part of the attempt by Rutger's to give them some sort of existence, in the hopes that someday the technology would become feasible to bring the eventual millions back to life into a safer and better world.

Several societal theorists opposed these measures, claiming it was a waste of resources. The genetic tree of humanity allowed for anyone's life to be re-created without a need for the original data and criticized that the plan itself implemented no proven way to restore the original personalities once they were brought back to life.

The counterargument was what exactly would constitute the personality of an individual? It was already proven that memories could be put back into the minds of individuals, whether real or not, whether theirs or not. The alleged 'crime' of the movement itself was another hotly debated ideology which did nothing to stop it.

However, Rutgers managed to maintain the support of sympathetic individuals within the movement. Anything they could do, no matter how faulty, could provide some benefit to people and the future. Jake had been one of these.

He joined Rutger's plan years ago and had proven both his

loyalty and support of the growing regime. Though opposed to its overall mission, he was aware of the rising tide of public sentiment, and shifted his focus to what he thought he could do.

Soon, the hologram of Emily flickered into focus. The years had been kind to Emily, her blonde hair was long, her face had filled out over time, and she remained as beautiful to Jake as she always had been, inside and out. She worked with Melissa, helping her develop a successful confectionery business. Emily spent most of her time connecting with the public and keeping on top of the orders for the company.

Emily looked over at Jake.

"Why is everything... blue?" she asked.

"I don't know, Emily." Laughing, he shrugged, "Try changing some of the settings."

Her brow furrowed. "Now I can't see you at all," she said, exasperated. She fiddled with the controls, "The leaves on those trees were red?"

"You got it," Jake said.

"I can hear what's going on around you. It's okay now," she said after a moment.

Jake turned and looked around the area. "Yeah, it only took a few weeks for the trees to get that way," he said.

"They're wonderful."

A group of people were walking down the pathway towards the main building, underneath the arch-ways constructed a few months prior.

"Can they see me?" Emily asked him.

"Yeah, I'm sure they can. They can't hear you, though. Here, come this way," and Jake started walking off the path through the courtyard.

"Will they walk through me?" Emily asked, nervously.

"They could, but not the projector you're using. Just move it towards me."

The image of Emily moved awkwardly towards Jake as she began to remotely operate the motorized projector.

"Jake!" Jake heard as someone split off and approached the two.

"Hey, Olin," Jake said.

"I've been wanting to see one of those projectors in action," Olin said. "Can you raise the projector, please?" he asked Emily.

Emily looked at Olin and then at Jake bewildered.

"Can she hear me, Jake?" Olin said.

"I can hear you," Emily said.

Olin looked back at the image. "There should be two settings for the audio, one for audio going into the projector, one for audio coming out."

"Can you hear me?" Emily's tinny voice came from the device projecting her image.

"Yeah, that's great! There you go," Olin said encouragingly, then looked at Jake standing impatiently next to him.

Emily looked back at Jake, then Olin. "Thank you," she said. "This is kind of giving me a headache, there's so much to learn," she said to Olin.

Olin looked at Jake awkwardly again. "I don't know why he didn't explain how it works to you."

"It's okay," Emily said. "If I get to use one of these again, I'll be sure to try and learn how to operate it better," she said.

Olin looked puzzled, then grinned.

"Well, it's still nice to see those old projectors being used. I hate to see someone having trouble with them, it gives a bad impression." Olin waved to Jake. "Take care, guys."

"New technology, Jake?" Emily said, and grinned.

Jake looked back at the image of Emily. "I was not supposed to send you that kit at all," he said. "I'm not supposed to have this projector."

They walked a good distance away from the courtyard and Jake turned back to the image of Emily.

"Have you heard about the Anarchists lately?" Jake asks. "They're saying everything is happening because the world is going to end."

"I know," Emily says. "I understand why they're saying it but I don't know what good it will do." Her eyes grow dark and she nervously adjusts her dress. "Everyone's trying to do the best they can with what's going on," she says and sighed.

"I want you to see something. This is why I needed you to

come out here like this," Jake says. "I don't know if you're going to be able to see this clearly through the projector, but it might work."

Bringing a small display device out of his pocket, he holds it up for her to see. "I rigged this up to hold vids, can you see it?"

The display shows a recent public rally of Anarchists with several speakers trying to gain support for the movement. Their message was confusing. They offered no solutions for the problems many were facing, they seemed to be saying what everyone already knew and felt. Their 'doom and gloom' message was understood, but not well received, as the crowd hurled insults and shouts at the speakers.

"I don't want to watch this," Emily said, "Why are you showing me this?"

"Just look at the screen. Look here," he says and points to a part of the display.

There were several people trying to speak to the crowd.

"It's hard to see, Jake," she said.

"I think this is Kevin," he says, indicating a figure towards the back.

Emily pauses. "Are you sure, Jake?"

"I think it's Kevin," he says. Nodding, he puts the device away.

"Just get rid of the kit," Jake says. "I've already covered why it's missing, I'll take care of the projector."

"Ok," Emily says. "It was good to see you again."

"You too," he replies.

The cargo vehicle slowly pushed through the throng of people that were banging on its sides. They cursed the people inside, praised the people inside, shouted to be let in, or shouted for them to die. They were terrified, as were also the men and women inside.

Gavril turns to Aaron. "It's not helping us that they know where we are, or where we will be."

"I know," Aaron replies with a shrug.

The members of Rutger's movement, the 'Plan of

Indoctrination', were doing everything they could to disrupt the mission of the Anarchists.

"Just keep driving," Aaron said.

Gavril clenched his fists and continued driving the vehicle.

Although slow at first, the vehicle finally made its way through the crowd, or maybe the crowd had simply given up. The purple and black night sky opened up to a world of collapsed buildings surrounding overgrown landscapes and brightly illuminated habitations and forests.

Gavril sniffed loudly and said to the others, "I'm going to turn off most of the power in here, but they might still be able to follow us. Stay calm."

A loud explosion suddenly blew the vehicle over and the passengers inside were thrown out of their seats against the inside of the vehicle.

Gavril yelled.

With the vehicle flipped over, their way out was above them. Reaching up, one of the passengers was able to open the door, while somewhere near the back another way was opened, giving everyone inside a second escape.

Waiting outside were armed men wearing black utility armor bearing a red half-circle on the chest, each holding a rifle at the emerging passengers. Stepping forward, one man said loudly, "Everyone! Lie down on the ground and we will not kill you. You will be brought to the local registration building to be preserved. Lie down on the ground and we will not kill you."

Several men and women, who had been convinced that Gavril and Aaron and his group offered an alternative out of the nightmare of the world, bent down to lie on the ground and comply with the wishes of the armored men.

Inside the vehicle, Gavril reached into his coat to retrieve his weapon. Aaron placed his hand on his arm, "Stay still," Aaron said quietly.

A few of the men and women chose to stay inside the vehicle, watching as those who had left were rounded up and taken inside another transport.

Afterward, the armed men approached the overturned vehicle, but didn't attempt to enter it. They conferred among themselves and upon reaching some agreement, they went back to the vehicles and left.

"They won't take us," Aaron said to the others. "Stay close."

"I'll call another transport," Gavril said, waiting to see if the soldiers would return. He pointed at the opening and said to Kevin, "Take a look and see if you can get us out."

Kevin pulled himself up to the opening and quickly rolled over the edge to hit the ground. He counted silently in his mind as he lay still. No sounds were heard and he lifted himself off the ground and cautiously sat up and saw a large translucent transport tunnel score an illuminated arc across the dark black sky. Below it was the dome they had left, bright from within. The transport tunnel connected at the top of a large platform and was built into the translucent wall of the dome itself.

A loud siren began to blare and Kevin rose to his feet. Rutger's men were rounding up the inhabitants in the area. He could see a few fires spreading out among the people and dwellings inside the dome. Twisted and tortured shapes, Kevin recognized some of the modifications given to the Warrior Caste as they waved their weapons, and Rutger's pacifist soldiers were attempting to round up those willing to submit.

There was no one in the immediate area, and Kevin turned to the inside of the transport. The passengers inside looked out at him through gray and dark shadows faintly lit through the panel lights. Kevin was surprised at how calm they were, given what they had just been through.

"It's safe," he said.

CHAPTER 20

"Death."

"Who?"

The room was dark and Aaron adjusted the metallic, fitted 'gauntlet' that served as a cheap bio read-out. The cubed blue light that rose from the back of the unit slowly lifted and wisped outwards as it began to illuminate the room.

In the darkness, golden irises quietly shined, its pale, misshapen cheekbones and chin were obscured with a long and taloned hand. It's thick and long tail reflexively curled.

"Turn it off," the figure said, retreating into the darkness.

"I've already activated it--" Aaron spoke before the room flashed a blinding white.

"Are you awake, Aaron?"

Aaron groggily moved his arms and lifted his head from the soft, feathery down, and light, silky fabrics he was prone upon. He looked out into a pale pink sky with three blazing suns, blue, purple and yellow. The three suns were different sizes, the blue one being far more immense than Aaron could comprehend all at once.

In the distance, tall spires reached higher than he was able to see. Balconies encircled each spire, bright orange and red, and it was on one of these that he was trying to stand. Another balcony above him finished the pavilion.

A pale white and muscled human figure stood in profile,

askance before the endless pink sky. It was encased in tightly fitting blue fabric, hidden under a curtain of sheer and gauzy silk that hung from its shoulders. Hovering around his neck, a circle of dimly lit black stones circled, resonating with an eerie light.

The figure looked up from its hands.

"Death, Aaron?"

"That's what they call you," Aaron said, rising to his feet and pulling his wits together through habit. "That's what they told me to call you. They said to call you Death," he said again as he struggled to hold his balance with the figure in his view. The endless void of pink vacuum pulled at his soul and his knees shook under him.

If he still had been wearing the metal gauntlet that served as his cheap bio read-out, it would be sending alarms for a pacifier as his heart beat thunderingly. He dropped to his knees and planted his hands on the ground.

Trying to calm himself, he realized the device was missing.

"Death it is, good."

Reaching its yellow and thickly taloned hand into the air, it stretched it's thick and heavy tail. Involuntarily, Aaron stumbled backward beginning to tremble uncontrollably.

"Good," he cooed again. Death turned its face towards Aaron, and Aaron struggled to remember this figure was a man just as he.

"Good," Death said a final time and began taking long strides towards Aaron. Aaron scrambled backward clawing at the fabric around him, saliva involuntarily running down his chin in an absolute, stark terror.

A cry of exultation rang out from the balcony. Three other figures on other balconies kept their intense concentration out onto the endless pink sky.

They were all Death as well.

"You know, Kevin, the word is that we can plug into quite a bit now," Starman said.

"Please leave me be," Kevin thought.

"You want to be left alone. Have a wonderful day!"

Starman, an artificially intelligent neural stabilizer, faded out of awareness and Kevin did his best to ignore the feelings that came from the years he had spent in Rutger's 'machine-world'.

He ran fingers through his mop of hair, lingering briefly over a plug behind his right ear. He shivered.

"You coming, Kev?" a voice yelled from behind a metal panel, one of the few authorized entrances to the bunker.

"Yeah, hold on," Kevin replied.

He heard rapid banging on the door. "Let's do this!" the voice said.

Alright, Aris, Kevin thought, and he almost grinned.

"We're about done hooking you up," Kevin heard on his left side.

"Alright," Kevin said after some time. A white and metallic robotic arm lowered and pressed an air mask to his face.

"You know what to do, Kevin. Take a deep breath," the voice of Aris said and Kevin thought again about how much he disliked the mask holding his head down and obscuring his vision. He was no longer able to see Aris or the others in the viewing room as they watched and analyzed various graphs and numbers, biological readouts giving anything from how strong Kevin's heartbeat was to the temperature of the room.

Kevin had learned the science he'd studied at University years ago had been 'worthless junk science'. Aris suspected it was deliberately taught to the students in an effort to be misleading without arousing suspicion. The principles behind the scientific theories Kevin could explain seemed backed by a 'religious propaganda style ideology', or so Aris had said to him. He enjoyed talking with Aris about what Aris liked to call 'thinking', Tanya called 'philosophy' and also 'a headache'.

"You've got a knack for it, Kev," Aris said.

"Concentrate on your breathing, Kevin," he heard Tanya's voice say through a speaker as he listened to the slight, tell-tale hissing sound. The brackets around his arms and legs latched and bolted.

"Oh, good! Don't worry, we almost got it, Kevin!" he heard

Tanya say, but the voice was far away. Another room. Not here, not now.

Slightly relieved, he breathed out cautiously and tasted something he couldn't identify in the air. Seventy-two particles of dust, fust, must. He breathed in again, his smile and eyes opened to white and gold light and sparks, a splash of crimson flew across his vision. Who?

I've never really understood consciousness, Kevin had said.

Me either but that's okay, it's me, it's me, he said.

A torrent of wet and cold ice crashed down on his body, but his warmth kept him alive.

I'm me, I'm me, I'm okay.

Sober reality swept across his face and gut like one long digging knife.

"Kevin? Kevin, are you alright?" Aris was saying.

"What?" Kevin was trying to be angry but found nothing to be angry with. He found empty nothing as his source of anger. His mind desperately clutched at an unyielding vacuum.

"I am trying to be angry?" He felt dizzy. "No, I mean, I'm trying to be angry," his words trailed off.

The voice of Aris came through the speaker tinny, brittle, and high pitched. Kevin felt pressure against his ear and the hairs on his body prickled and stood on end.

"We're almost done adjusting everything. You're a champion, Kevin. Just hold it together, man," he heard Aris say.

A taste of burnt, dark caramel lingered in his nose and mouth. Kevin was breathing normally again.

He woke up hours later, briefly, and learned the operation had finished well. The device used to 'upload' him to the shared and synthetic reality Rutger's was using to preserve the population had been removed and could now be accessed with the Anarchist's technology. One down, Kevin thought.

"You're doing a great thing," he heard Aris mention.

Kevin wondered how close he'd been to losing his life.

A little each day, Kevin would awaken for a few hours, but he spent most of his time sleeping through recovery. He was in a complex controlled by the Anarchists. Originally a warehouse for ship parts, it now housed stolen equipment scavenged from the Old Empire's plantation in South America. The plantation itself was now almost entirely under the authority of the remaining members of the Bio's Caste.

Word had it, from Tanya, that the Bio's Caste had closed their ranks, denying all others the rights for membership, the ability to learn the information, knowledge, and secrets they held.

Tanya, formerly of the Bio's Caste, explained the Bio's Caste was no longer allowing access to the plants they held within Old Empire and this was a bad omen for the rest of the world.

The Bio's, in the old days, before the August plantation on the other continent, before even the Armored Wing near the Great Lakes, had studied the effects of gaze on the body and learned its secrets. They learned to manipulate a simple leaf from which gaze was produced, and the subsequent forms that allowed those who needed gaze to survive.

This had all been new information to Kevin, who had a very different understanding of the world, Tanya thought. He was born in one the plantations, raised on lies and propaganda, with the false belief the Empire was a sovereign nation fighting a terrible war with defectors. What Tanya found most surprising was that Kevin was raised with hope.

Tanya shook her head and still tried to put away the idea that those raised with Kevin, raised inside the Militia Wing plantation, were all similar to him. They believed in peace, and Avena, another idea started and supported by the Vision Caste. Most profoundly, they believed in the Empire itself, which had produced the substance that tied the lives of so many together into a war with no name, no voice, a blind world suffering from a blind war, with no clear victory, that these children believed and even held on to some type of seeming innocence that the world could be made into a better place, that there was an answer to be found somewhere, if one only looked hard enough for it.

Aris, on the other hand, believed it was more a product of Kevin's youth coupled with the lies the Militia Wing had used to control the population and maintain power. He did not think the Vision Caste believed the ideas they peddled to the masses, because none of their actions could be seen as a solution to the world's current crisis. Avena was nothing more than an illusion perpetrated by the Vision Caste to help embed their lies even further. They both agreed it would get much worse before it ever got better.

Prominent members of the Empire remained silent when Rutger's began his movement, as it was a way to capture and erase those born without access to gaze, no longer needing to enslave those without power, but allowing the world a new norm where those without power owed their lives to those that had it.

It was a conversation many fell ill with when probing Aris too deeply about his views, even Aaron. The primitive, nonsensical meaning behind things, as Aaron would say, had stopped bothering him, and he was able to speak with Aris without anger. A cool rationale, as Aris and Tanya put it.

Aris, and Aaron, had agreed that some admired and honored those with immortality and power. Most lived their lives through fear. It did not matter that the state of the world did not make sense, but this mattered to Aris, and his life was about fighting things that did not make sense.

Aaron had aptly pointed out to Aris that maybe Aris was afraid when things didn't make sense.

Aris replied it no longer mattered to him what made him fearful. If he could still recognize the difference between sense and nonsense, his fear meant nothing if he could do something about it.

CHAPTER 21

Rick shuddered and a loose paper caught on his jacket as he slept.

Atop a star and far below it, through the air and above the snow, trailing along placid waters, calm had settled behind the storm.

Paper was common in the city he lived in.

"Never fear," a robin said, darting sprightly limb from limb.

"What's over here?" sang another, hopping on a whim.

Beds were not.

Rick lifted his head and pulled a corner of his cotton jacket up to his eyes to clean them. He would need to find a way to get some 'slime' today, a type of thick cleaning gel. His body was dirty, he seldom slept inside.

He knew he would be able to eat today. This gave him the strength to try and get clean, the strength and ability to adjust his routine, and possibly even find a new place to sleep at night.

Life in this city was not easy for Rick. He had branded himself as an orphan which allowed him to pick up food at an orphan shelter once or twice a week, and it also gave him some privileges with various groups in the area. He wasn't able to work for anyone. Choosing to be branded an orphan prevented his citizenship and right to work. He was allowed to leave the city and join whatever was going on somewhere else, but here in Mexcatl an orphan was orphan for life.

He thought he might be able to trade some of his rations for some credit.

Then he thought he might be able to use some of the credit and get drunk.

"Fuck this," Rick thought.

He had been unable to get back to Militia Wing and had given up on returning some time ago. He seldom thought of it, there was nothing to think about. He had been abandoned. Kevin had disappeared and Emily, Jake, and Rick had gone their separate ways, but not before Rick had given Jake a piece of his mind.

Suddenly, Rick felt a sharp kick to his ribs.

"Get up," the voice said.

"Hey, what--"

"Now! Get up!"

Rick tried to push himself to his feet.

"Hands where I can see them," the voice said.

Fuck, Rick thought. He was brought up to his feet and pushed with his chest against the wall. His arms were pulled backward.

"Hey!" Rick exclaimed.

"You're no longer allowed in this city," the voice said.

Clamps were placed around his hands and he could no longer use them. Trying to move his arms away from each other, the clamps burned his hands with electricity. He howled in pain and a billy club was brought to the back of his skull and he fell to the ground.

"You're a fucking scumbag," the guard said.

"I didn't do anything!" Rick yelled.

"It doesn't mean shit now, dirtbag. Get up!" He was kicked once more, and then finally allowed to get back to his feet. He had kept his hands close together as he pushed himself up. He'd never felt such terrifying pain in his hands before. They no longer felt shocked, but the pain lingered agonizingly and his fingers felt dead.

"What did I do?" Rick pleaded to his attacker.

"Doesn't mean shit now, fucker."

He was brought to the back of a vehicle, tagged, and

committed. He would later learn that his crime was the murder of another citizen of Mexcatl. It hadn't mattered whether he was guilty or innocent. They were ending the orphan program. They were canceling everything in the city. Most of the citizens were being rounded up for preservation. Those that had been found guilty of criminal acts were not eligible. Rick was an orphan. He was useless, he was not eligible.

He was not alone.

"Aris?" came Tanya's voice from the entryway.

"Over here, hun."

Tanya spied Aris through the mass of cables and boxes, and Aris privately thought about the old adage beauty in art, taking in her red haired beauty once more. He went lightheaded, his heart betrayed him, still.

Tanya was bred in Old Empire, her beauty the engineered work of the Bio's caste. She was a Bio herself, which meant, aside from a scripted beauty, she knew more secrets about the human condition than Aris could ever hope to understand in several lifetimes.

It made his work seem ludicrous, but it was Tanya's support that gave Aris the hope he was gaining ground in advancing the cause which pulled together so many followers. While they were making progress and moving forward, they struggled to convince the population something could be done about their fate. Ending the Empire was the first and most vicious strike against the ruling status quo.

Rutger's movement, this so-called 'Plan of Indoctrination', had confused those willing to take on the label of Anarchist and it blurred their message to the remaining world.

Knowledge and access to gaze, brought in through various Grippers and confirmed through studies of the substance itself, helped in convincing new recruits, but now it seemed they were fighting a two-sided war, and through this, they were losing not only the means to convince others but their morale and the support.

An illusion of power was one of the primary tools of the Anarchists. Aris, being a de facto leader, a leader through thought and idea, had learned to quell his own misgivings about using illusion as a means to an end. He knew he must always make the Anarchists seem more powerful than they were.

The basilisk born of the cold and dead egg, the rooster would crow. The symbol of Aris' group was a crowing cock against the backdrop of the old moon. The scars on the planet from the strike against the moon were well known, even by this late stage in mankind's progress, and its rain of ruin upon the earth had collapsed the ecosystem.

Earth was a swamp, though large swatches of arid and drier land still existed. Tanya possessed a developed immunity to the more terrible parts of Earth's environment, Aris was not as lucky. His surface veins were a pale ochre color under his dull skin. His dark black hair had been pigmented to reflect a violet light.

Aris was running numbers through a calculator, trying to understand how much more gaze was needed, how many of those loyal to the anarchists needed it, and anxious over how to secure it.

"Have you seen Aaron, Aris?" Tanya asked. She laid her fingertips against his arm.

Aris looked up. "Not since I gave him the new neuralyzers, why?"

"He hasn't taken gaze in several days, Aris," Tanya said.

Aris looked up sharply. "Where is his room?"

"Not far," she said.

Rick stood in line with his tray, waiting for his food. He ate more than before, probably too much, and slept on a bed each night. The workers down here piled on the feeling of doom and guilt higher and higher as he eyed the mound of stewed vegetation, stewed protein lumps, stewed anything.

"It's good for the digestion," a large man with fiery eyes told him from behind the protected see-through wall. He smiled.

"The more cooking that goes into the food, the more nutrients, the easier it is for the stomach to absorb," he said and grinned again. The man was large, his girth was sheathed in a white apron, a simple cafeteria uniform. His face moved with the tell-tale signs of neurological alteration.

He was a prisoner, as was Rick.

The man, behind the wall, eyed the food again and his mouth curved to a prim and tight-lipped grin.

"Good food," he said.

Rick carried the burden with him to a table with four others and tried to sit without giving it another thought. He knew more would join, and soon enough, two or three others sat down near to him, their stale body odor mixed with the smell of filth, a smell that clung to the inside of the nostrils. One of the men started eating hungrily and another eyed Rick in a way indicating he was about to talk and the others avoided Rick.

"Are you going to eat all that?" the man asked. Rick already felt guilty.

"Yeah," Rick said, looking down at his tray and he lifted some of the gloppy stew into his mouth.

"Is it good?" the man said sharply.

Rick didn't look up. "Yeah, it's good."

The man beside Rick was still noisily shoveling food into his mouth and Rick was grateful. After a moment of quiet, the other man began to eat as well and Rick kept his eyes down.

Sitting at the corner of the table, a man who looked like he belonged where they were, looked sidelong at Rick with a utensil in his hand and, while chewing, asked quietly, "Are you new here?"

The man to Rick's left paused in his eating before hurriedly beginning to eat again.

"Look, leave me alone, alright?" Rick almost whispered.

"Be quiet," a reddish-haired man said quickly.

Rick swallowed and looked back down at his food.

"You weird?" the reddish-haired man said after taking another measured bite.

"Don't say anything," the man across the table from Rick said, before returning back to eat.

"You weird?" the man with the red clay colored hair asked again.

Angrily, Rick said, "I don't know what you mean." He noticed the young man, who had asked him about his meal, was studying him with a worried expression.

"You weird? You're weird if you know it," the man said quietly and laughed, and his face shifted between a type of happiness and sadness. "You're weird, you know it," he said again. He began repeating his statement, until his hands shook as he tried to eat again.

"You've done it now," the man to Rick's left said and suddenly seemed in a hurry to finish his meal.

"Not good," the other one said, the one across the table.

The man was growing more agitated and suddenly flipped his tray upwards into the air and slammed his hands down on the table and bellowed loudly, food splattering everywhere.

"You-- God! Fuck me! Hell!" the man yelled haltingly over the words.

"Angels!" the man yelled and started banging his hands loudly against the table.

The man to Rick's right scraped the remaining food on his tray into his mouth and sprung up off the table. Rick barely had time to notice the boy across the way mouth 'get up' to him before leaping away from the table.

Rick stood up, and the red clay colored haired man looked at him and they locked eyes.

"The boy with the candle," the red-haired man said suddenly.

In Rick's mind, a fire raged. For a brief moment, he had a feeling that he remembered this.

"The boy with the flame," the red clay colored haired man said again, before bellowing out loudly and slamming his hands on the table again.

"Come on," the older man said to Rick, pulling him away from the table.

"Get to the wall, come on," he said.

The rest of the men in the room were lining up against the walls, leaving the bellowing man yelling loudly at the top of his lungs and slamming his hands on the table. Activity and commotion started behind the see-through and protected walls.

"What's he doing?" Rick said through the noise as a loud alarm began to ring.

"He's trying to prove he's crazy," the older man said.

"What?"

"He's trying to get out of here," the man said as they both stood still with their face and chest against the wall.

"You can get out of here?" Rick asked.

"No, but if you're crazy they will keep you by yourself," the man said. "It won't work though, not with him."

"Why?" Rick asked. They ignored him for a moment.

"We all know that man is crazy, we've all known," the younger man said, the one who had asked about Rick's meal.

"So?" Rick asked as he turned to look back at the one man in the room still sitting at a table.

"They won't keep you around if there's something wrong with you," the young man said again.

"What do you mean?" Rick asked.

"He's got something wrong with him," the other man said.

As the alarm continued to ring, the light in the room grew red and a black, evil whine began keening in the air.

"Yep," the younger boy muttered bitterly.

The man in the red clay colored uniform slumped at the table, fell to the floor.

"What?" Rick asked.

"He's dead," one of them said. "They killed him."

After a moment, he added, "They kill the ones like that."

"Poor fuck," the skinny man said.

"Wasn't he crazy?" Rick said.

"Like I said, they don't do anything with you if you really are crazy," the older man said.

"Poor fucking bastard," the skinny young man muttered again.

"Eat your food, don't talk to anyone," the dark colored man said to Rick.

As they were exiting the cafeteria, single file, the older man behind Rick said, "If you got a chance to tell them you're cuckoo, do it."

"Won't they do that to me?" Rick whispered forcefully.

"Not unless you really are," the older said and he laughed.

Rick awoke on a bed in a room of beds with sleeping prisoners. The inmates, trustees, guards and some of the more intelligent within the administration, those within the prison who were not altogether committed, called the prison 'the Maze'.

It was a sprawling, labyrinthine environment put together in a ramshackle fashion, construction delegated to various groups by those in power of Mexcatl and the surrounding areas, put together by various groups at differing times. It was a camp, in a way, for the ne'er-do-wells of society, the criminal outcasts, the dangerous, and others not needed by society.

Much of the equipment for the prison came as donations and security was enforced through the threat of death. There was no political recourse for inmates, there was no action to take should you feel your treatment unfair.

There was one option, after enough time, and that option was to die. Dying was usually a solution offered or presented for any problems one should face inside the Maze. Die, or ask to die. One less mouth to feed, one more bed freed up for the next.

The administration spoke of 'being released', but Rick soon realized it was a farcical understanding, no one left the Maze, there was no exit, and Rick felt this to be sadly ironic. He assumed the administration muttered to themselves over their good humor, their wittiness in cleverly outwitting the slack and mentally dull or absent convicts.

Rick opened his eyes, hearing the entry to the room had opened. A soft light appeared, bringing with it a bit of fresh air to make its way circuitously through the haze of old, death and the release from fear.

"A-415, Collins," the voice called. It was Rick. It was Rick's name and number.

"Yeah," Rick called out sleepily, afraid to show signs of life, afraid to show any emotion, mute and neutral, just a prisoner, just another unwilling soul to greet the day, clearly at the mercy of circumstances beyond his control, and just as willingly resigned to his fate. The years in Mexcatl had taught him everything quick enough.

It was late into the night.

"A-415, come this way," the voice said again.

Rick pulled himself out of the bed, careful not to make any noise, and followed the figure through the tunnel that allowed access to the prisoner's sleeping rooms. They were large spaces, much of the secure parts of the complex were underground, the rooms had been hollowed out of the earth and cemented and fiber-blasted.

The beds for the prisoners were aligned in rows and chained down. There was no protection offered, as there was no real fear for the death of an inmate. Both the assailant and victim would reach the same fate. One loss of life enforced, one life stolen, respectively.

The man in front of Rick was strangely subdued and silent as Rick followed him down the aged tan and gray colored hallway. The smell of earth leaked through cracks in the housing.

He brought Rick to a door and rested his palm against a sensor near to it. Rick noticed another antiquated locking system as well.

The door opened and the man nodded to Rick. He looked inside to a small young boy, sitting at a long table with chairs scattered about. It looked like a meeting place that had been abandoned and eventually used for storage. There was no rhyme or reason to its organization, things were simply placed where they were left and more than likely, and inevitably or eventually, forgotten.

The little boy smiled at Rick. "Have a seat, please."

Rick looked at the guard next to him, holding the door, and the guard's mouth slightly smiled as he vaguely looked at Rick and then continued staring out into nothing. His eyes showed no sign of a human recognition and Rick only became aware of this phenomenon having just witnessed it. To the guard, Rick might as well have been a poster board cut-out with as much activity as the man's face and mannerism showed. The guard's eyes were vaguely oriented toward the young boy.

"Thank you, Malcolm," the boy said to the guard. "Please stand outside and listen carefully, if you don't mind."

The guard's eyes seemed to focus and he straightened up.

He seemed as if he would turn and exit the room, then slacked again, hand resting on the door. Rick gingerly walked by him and hesitated, then after making a decision, decided to move closer to the table and the boy.

The young boy's brow furrowed in concentration. "If you stand outside the door, you can hear if there's any trouble inside and you can come in and help," the boy said.

The man's mouth slightly opened and he slowly pulled himself to attention as if moving through jelly.

"Alright," the man said after some time and his eyes grew dull again.

The boy waited patiently and served Rick with a glance of mock frustration.

"You can do it now," the boy said after a moment.

The guard stood silently as if waiting. Rick thought he heard the guard slowly humming to himself, though it could have been the ambient noise of the room.

"Go," the boy said.

The guard slowly turned and then left the room.

"Close the door behind you, Malcolm," the boy said.

The latch closed with an audible click.

Rick stayed looking down at the blonde haired little boy and the little boy turned his dark brown eyes up to meet Rick's.

Sit down, the little boy thought in Rick's head.

Rick slowly sat down in a chair. His mouth hung slack, his eyes wide on the boy's soulful smile.

"This is not the end, Rick," the boy said with his smile, and reached a hand out to grab Rick's wrist. "This is not what you think it is, but I do not want you to fear," the boy said looking into Rick's eyes.

"Watch the flame," the boy said while holding Rick's wrist. Rick's arm remained in the air of its own accord. Rick was afraid to move it, but it seemed maybe his autonomous system held it rigid and in place, as the young boy simply wrapped his palm around his wrist.

In the boy's other hand, a flame appeared, as he held his hand out flat and vertical.

A moment of recognition flickered in Rick's mind and he

felt claws sink into his yielding and tensile consciousness.

"You knew," said the boy.

Death pulled his talons out from Rick's mind, like a syringe being removed from skin, and a paper doll cut-out of Kevin, Jake and Emily appeared in the void that surrounded them.

"Don't mind, Rick. Please don't mind," the little boy said from far off.

Rick sensed the talons of Death flicker over Emily, Kevin, then Jake. Check marks. Recognition.

Rick shivered and the flame in the boy's little hand wavered. The boy did not let go of Rick's wrist and Rick remained frozen, staring with rapt concentration.

Death stepped out from behind Rick, and the scene on the table, the prison and the little boy, faded into vertigo, and nothing surrounded Rick and Death but white light.

"Don't worry about it, Rick, there's no reason to be alive by this point. The odds won," Death remarks. His arm waves dramatically across the broad white nothing and splashes of color form a blue landscape, with pristine green meadows, while mountains fall from the sky, and the sun shines brightly. The moon, larger than ever, appears like chalk, pale blue and white.

At a notion from Rick, a whisper inside of him, a voiceless desire, an ocean appears and the call of birds ring out.

"There is this, and more of what you want," Death mutters, looking away. Looking over at Death, his eyes avert and slide off the dark figure.

"At the moment, I am speaking with your friend Aaron, who will speak with several people, including your childhood friend, Kevin, but it's not important."

Rick shivers again as he tries to think of the room he's supposed to be in, the little boy, but it's nothing but a faded memory.

"This might as well be as real as anything out there," Death says. "I was a little boy as well, Rick. Once. Only once, maybe. Though I suppose it doesn't always work out that way," he says, coming into focus clearly for the first time.

His frame is a skeleton, his face bone, with blue textured

sparks or veins running the length of his smoky gray face. He wears a cowl and hood.

"I borrowed this image from history. It is fearful."

"I am not old. I am 19, Rick," Death says.

"I was grown," Death says and smiles. "We were grown. A project, the four of us."

Rick's eyes begin to brim with tears.

"I don't know why," Rick says, and he chokes and sobs.

"Don't worry, Rick, it's normal, you are having the normal response," and Death lets out a sigh. "They knew when they made us that the world was not big enough for us. That was the intention from the outset, it seems."

The pastoral and panoramic view slides from vision and Rick finds himself sitting at a dusty table, the smell of earth bleeding in through the cracks, and the little blonde haired boy sitting at the table, still holding Rick's hand.

"Did you see him?" the boy asks.

"I did," Rick says after a moment.

The little boy closes the flame in his palm.

"Good," he says and lets go of Rick's wrist. "If I study real hard, I am able to do this," the little boy says, meaning the flame in his hand.

CHAPTER 22

Kevin stood on a stage with equipment that rendered images for the rest of the large room to see.

This part of the Anarchist's headquarters was used as an auditorium and those loyal to the Anarchists, even those not loyal to the Anarchists, were crowding around speaking with each other in subdued tones.

Aris was growing bolder in his statements and message.

"... the Avena towers are being constructed as a type of energy portal to allow small groups of people, or even larger groups, to be transported from tower to tower, instantaneously."

"How many is 'large', Aris?" one of the men from the crowd asked, over the chatter, while some of the other men laughed.

Aris waved his hand in the air. "More than 10, let's say."

"How does it work, how did you get this information?"

The data transfer finished for the visual equipment in the room, various technical information and model renderings of one of the Avena towers glowed quietly in front of them.

"That's not important right now, just listen to me!" Aris said loudly.

"What are you leading us into, Aris?"

"What has any of this got to do with bringing down the Empire?" another shouted, and the clamor in the room began to pick up in volume.

"Please, listen," Aris said, walking over to the other side of the visual equipment and moving the images along until a bird's eye view of the tower's network was shown in its place.

"Three of the towers are fully operational, it's more or less a transit system."

As the room began to quiet down, Kevin looked sharply at Gavril, and Gavril subtly nodded. Both Kevin and Gavril knew Aris would not reveal all of the information they had gathered from Aaron.

"What is it for, Aris?" said one of the men.

Aris turned outwards and faced the group. "Well, think about it," he said. "The travel is instantaneous and it transports living as well as material cargo, from what we can gather."

The various people began talking among themselves and Kevin couldn't help but try and wonder.

"It's for undetectable transport," Aris finished. Aris walked over to one of the men in the room and slapped him on the shoulder. "I'll say it for you," Aris announced. "The Empire has found a way to transport people and probably material goods outside of detection"

The tone in the room began to shift and Aris walked across the room, no longer leader, just another scientist characteristically excited by a new discovery.

"Can they move an army, Aris?" a voice called out.

"Not according to these diagrams, Kalor," Aris replied.

Gavril spoke up. "We believe the intent behind the tower network is to safely transport important individuals, documents, and other valuable items, instantaneously, with no fear of detection by any other parties."

"Did they get this technology from Avena?" a voice called. There was an uncomfortable laughter that did little for the tension in the room.

"Quite possibly," Aris said. "We need to get men in front of this network. We need to get some of them to be our men."

Kevin sighed to himself and surveyed the crowd. Gavril was gone, and Kevin quietly left as well. It was what Aris wasn't saying. It was what Aris wasn't telling the crowd that mattered.

The Earth was a hogwash. The Earth was a no-go. Aris and the others had found another way out of this mess. They could leave the Earth and its problems behind. They wouldn't need to

stay on Earth and defend a dying planet any longer.
They had found a way out.
They had found Michael, and Michael had found Horizon.

CHAPTER 23

The new bio-rhythm Jen was under allowed her close to four hours of sleep for an enhanced mental stability. It allowed for dreams, without dreaming too deeply, and an overall feeling of rest throughout the day.

Jen was under monitoring and close supervision, because her biology was in a fragile state. She was older than the Empire.

"I had a dream about Michael Janice," Jen said after she awoke.

"Michael! He has been doing fine, Jen. Good as always."

"I wish they would let him out more," Jen said.

"We do too, Miss Lockard. We're working on it."

"When can I see him again?"

"Soon, now is not a good time. He is undergoing his procedure," was the reply.

"Oh, I worry for him," Jen stated. "I had a terrible dream about him."

Jen pushed a button inside her sleep capsule enabling a field of electronic privacy and turned on a broadcast channel.

As she lay back in the cool and dim environment, the broadcast's vivid colors streaked across the interior. She decided to ignore the visual input. Closing her eyes, the colors from the broadcast lit the inside of her eyelids and washed her retinas in a flickering light.

The chatter of the broadcast, Empire propaganda, and it was

always Empire propaganda, stated various happenings in different parts of the world. The segment was centered around persons of interest, mainly. She sighed and breathed deeply.

Again a talk of the importance of loyalty towards the Empire and, ultimately, Avena. Another stark and grim warning about the importance of loyalty and warning against defections. Another talk with leaders of various parts of Earth. Whispers of Anarchist uprisings, Anarchists among us, the importance of loyalty and adherence to the Empire.

Jen was a person of non-interest. She smiled. Her family was revered among the oldest of the Empire's members and Jen was the only remaining blood relative of the original family.

She remembered her father as a kind man. The void of Old Earth was filled with years that rushed together into the now, and it was the now she wished to focus on. She would push with Sen Jola for a visit with Michael. Her dream had been uncomfortable, but maybe if he listened, a flicker of his old personality would shine through.

They would have left Michael just as he was, Jen thought. Locked in a crystalline slumber, forever frozen the way he was, the way she was forever locked inside of her own body. The body she knew the way it was the night she had decided to take the fateful plant she had helped spread across the world.

The newer leaders, the ones recently introduced, had pushed for law and order to be established within the ruling powers of the Empire.

Originally, the struggling Vision Caste had sought to attain some type of purpose and direction to unite the crumbling powers and loyalties within the Empire, and they had found it with this story of Avena.

They were the new recruits, the fresh branding on the flank of the Casted, and their struggle to attain a type of law and order had been achieved. The Empire's introduction of stabilization had taken its measure of success, and the August plantation and its ruling body among the Vision Caste were lauded as the visionaries they were designed to be, leading many to consider the August plantation and the Vision Caste to be the Empire's ruling body, pro tempore.

She wondered how her father would have felt about the Empire as it was today. Jen's father had never decided to join the Empire in completion. Not when his health was failing, his eyes blind and his body deteriorating with age.

It was his wife, Linda, who succeeded him in directing the work he had left behind, and it was she who had introduced the wars and the birth pains which had given rise to the Empire Jen knew today. Jen had helped nurture the Bio's Caste into its place, by virtue of her to kinship to the Queen.

Jen stepped out of her sleep capsule. She was not the only one to have taken gaze during her later stages of development.

The Bio's Caste had achieved a great deal of knowledge over the ages and began to revolutionize and change the Empire's perception of the body and mind, of age and death, growth and life. She was 'old', but she did not mind. Despite the changes technology brought to life within the spectrum of humanity, there was still a desire to acknowledge the past, with or without the knowledge of what it truly was.

Her apartment was sweetly fragranced with newly flowering hyacinths, set into the interior niche of a wall. The light in the habitat and pristine and cultivated health of the flowers lent more warmth and a bit of coolness to the atmosphere. Stepping through a sliding door onto an open, wide balcony, she noted, yet again, how everything was clean, wonderfully colored and in order as she placed her hands upon the nearby sill.

Lost in thought, her dream came meandering into the back of her mind. Michael, in a deep and still lake, surrounded by blood flowing in from the shores. She felt she'd had this dream before.

Shaking herself out of revelry, she left the balcony and slid out of her apartment into the second story corridor of Building X-11. She walked briskly down the hallway passing Sen Kori's office, one of the chief officers of the project to try and re-institute Michael's personality. Morning sunlight illuminated the world outside through the side of the translucent wall to her right, as the corridor arced around the building.

She passed by a number of entrances to other apartments as

she continued to make her way, wondering why she'd had the dream at all.

"Good, I'm glad you're well, Ver Lockard."

Masen Kaplan used the honorific Ver when addressing Jennifer Lockard's social status. Masen itself was an honorific, the Ma- indicating he was able to give an order to another of his title. In Jordi Kaplan's case, this would indicate he was able to direct other Sens within the Empire.

A Sen was a fairly common occurrence, one simply needed the training to acquire the role of a Sen. It inferred an informal level of privilege, certain privacies, and was a rank involved in the more private or confidential matters within the ruling of the Empire.

Ver simply meant a person of familial honor and afforded no official privilege aside from whatever a party was willing to afford. Jen held no official role, she had once been a person of distinction, but had since retired from it. There was no Maver, as there were no official actions to be directed, though Jen supposed that if her father were still alive and held no other honorary position, he would be considered Maver.

By using this title to address Jen, Masen Kaplan was indicating he was allowed to enforce any official action with her he deemed appropriate, as was a customary greeting of a Masen.

Titles aside, Jen, as one of the founding members of the Bio's Caste, felt no pressure or paranoia from Kaplan, and rightly took the honor for what it was simply meant to be, a polite recognition of her status, a salute from one political comrade to the next.

"You were there for the Four Door project, weren't you, Jen?" Kaplan asked.

"The supermen project?"

"Yes. You Bios were trying to create a superhuman, push the envelope of human genetics to its limit, if you'll forgive a layperson's garbled metaphor."

"I had left the Bio's Caste by then, Jordi," Jen said delicately.

Masen Kaplen leaned closer and said in a conspiratorial

whisper, "They've not left that building they commandeered some ten years ago, Jen." Jen remained silent and Masen Kaplen continued, "After one of the brothers died. They never leave it."

"The project should have never taken place," Jen said quietly.

"It devastated those kids," Kaplen said, searching Jen Lockard's face and eyes.

He suddenly leaned back. "Well, there is no good of it now," he sighed, and placed his hands on the desk. "But there's this! I've gotten something from someone close to the project, I could have kept it to myself, but I'd like to get an opinion."

Kaplan cleared his throat and recited, "'Toby, I hope this missive finds you. I am with others now, most of them seem willing to believe in this false reality. Some will listen, but I think many of them think I am daft.'"

"'They're stating the place we were, where you still might be, is a false reality constructed by a man to bring them into a better future. They sound like you!'"

"'How far out does it go, Toby? The thought is striking. If I can reach you from this place, if others already know about the place where you are, then what is to say the believed reality here isn't anything more than a further illusion?'"

"'Do we really die, Toby? Some say that there are even some here who never die! That the gods, or technology, keeps them alive or that they have always been alive. What is this place?'"

"It goes on like this for a while," Kaplan states.

Jen looked at Masen Kaplan in confusion.

"Obviously it is someone speaking about the 'Plan of Indoctrination'," he said.

"The person seems unfamiliar with the Empire," Jen said after a moment.

"I know, that appears to be genuine. It would be rare if someone has made it out of Rutger's machinery, but not altogether surprising. Why it was handed to me by a contact with the Four Doors project, I don't understand."

"Can't you ask them?" Jen asked.

"No, not the way I received it," Kaplan replied. "Would you

like to see them?"

"Jordi, I'm actually here to see Michael."

Masen Kaplan's eyes turned dark. "I can't let you do that, Jen. Sen Jola has informed me no one is to interrupt the procedure from this point forward, and frankly, I'm with him on it."

Jen sighs deeply and Kaplan continues. "From what I gather, Michael is not in a good state, and you, of anyone, should be aware of what that means to the Empire. After Sen Jola shared some of the information with me, I don't believe I'm in a good position now," he says, looking hard at Jen with piercing eyes.

Jen nodded. "I understand, Masen Kaplan."

Silence filled the room until Kaplan spoke again. "Who was he, Jen?"

"He was a friend of my father's, Jordi," Jen replied.

"I suppose you're not going to tell me why he was in isolation for so long."

"I don't know, myself," she said.

The room hummed and beeped softly, and a call from a loudspeaker was heard in the distance. Masen Kaplen looked aside at the terminal on his desk and sighed. "Are you sure you don't want to see the boys? The invitation is open."

"Yes, I'd like that," Jen said.

CHAPTER 24

"There are a lot of different things to see in the world, it's impossible to see them all."

"I tell you, these boys have done it. They've seen everything."

"No."

"Yes. In their lifetime, all things."

"Come on, Benly."

"They must have! They've devoured all of the communications, channels they've established when they were seven, at one time in their lives these kids have completely known and seen absolutely everything, ever, that ever was and how it will be!"

"Hate to jam your signal, Benly, but we've got company."

A moment was taken to brush pastry crumbs from clothing.

"Now, Ver Lockard, just to let you know, they're much older than they were since the last time you were here," Metmal said, one of the research staff for Four Doors. Spider eyes hooked on a robotic camera came crawling along the ceiling.

"What are they doing here?" Jen asked.

"They can't stop moving, they can't stop thinking, they always have to be active."

"The boys have built so much, Ver Lockard, why don't you say 'Hi' to Dec, he's over behind you," Metmal said cheerfully. The researchers with Four Doors were usually left to themselves. They were pleasantly surprised at the company.

"Hi, Dec!" Jen turned to see a figure swimming through some kind of liquid, moving his head and waving his hand as he passed by, operating the dials inside of a box while turning slowly.

"He's underwater," she said, turning back to the researchers.

"Ven is in the other room, why don't you go in there?" Dec interrupted, his voice projecting outside of the water. Dec turned toward Jen and held out his arm in a vague direction towards an opening where Ven would surely be.

"Good idea," she said and smiled. He seemed frustrated, but she did not mind. She walked down to see Ven, beyond another corridor, beyond two other men who certainly served as friends and protection to the three, now, not four.

They were designed with the utmost limits in mind, when the Empire and the Bio's Caste were at the peak of their aristocracy, blazing forward a path filled with their complete understanding of simply just the biological knowledge that they possessed.

Those who dealt with them found each to be both enemy and friend all rolled up into one package never truly meant for the world, each with their own distinctions. Grotesque in one way, beautiful in another, they were super-human and hard to understand. Their creation revealed the nature of the Bio Caste's flawed and draconic superiority, the genetics that were guided and the principles that were followed. They were beautiful in a way that could never again be accomplished, terrifying in their heightened human visage, yet more than the Bio's Caste had ever hoped to accomplish. They were devastating, yet sought the usual needs and comforts common to all.

Initially registered to finish a design based on one of the Empire's preternatural philosophical thinkers, before the biological work of creating them had begun, they were built to pull together all the necessary pieces to bring into reality an architectural structure to house and feed millions without need of oversight.

It was to be self-guiding, using the inhabitants of the city to draw on for the living city to grow organically and creating laws established as part of an interconnected system.

At the age of 4, the boys were introduced to it, first rejecting the plan as flawed, only to quickly change course and design the city. They soon fell to squabbling over details and direction.

Masen Kaplen had informed Jen that after the death of Trig, one of the four, they began to construct the city.

"What brings you here? Dec and I are still working on Trion, how do you like living here?" Ven said.

"It's very nice, it's very wonderful, I did not know that you-- were responsible, Ven," Jen said.

"Dec and I," said Ven. "It's a modification of an older design, but we'll get it done," Ven said, moving between chairs and closing books.

Jen could not remember the name of which one of the four had died, so did not ask about the other brothers. The city Jen lived in, the architectural design of two, possibly three teenagers, was as brilliant as it was sad and despotic.

"It's lovely," she said, diplomatically.

They were people, just as you or I. They were human like us all.

CHAPTER 25

"An explosion. Twenty-three of them. They're Grippers."

The remaining brother, Kaid, manufactured the whole thing. He influenced the Grippers to attack Empire City and in doing so, freed Michael from his centuries-long imprisonment. With the Empire caving from within, Kaid discovered the information he needed and informed his two remaining brothers. With the use of gaze, Kaid was able to accomplish what the brothers had set out to accomplish.

Kaid found Rick, he found Jake, he found Aaron. Only Kaid spoke with them and he spoke with them as Death, as a figure.

In the short years of their lives, the brothers had built the city in which many of the Empire would call home.

There was no lie to these three. The lie was simply the truth concealed.

They wanted to end it all. They just wanted to end the show. The technology being used for the Avena Towers was so unstable that it had started to break down physical matter, a process that would eventually render the sun blind.

The three boys orchestrated events that allowed them to gain control of this process. At that moment, with the turn of a dial, the chain reaction was accelerated and in the span of a breath, it was gone.

In Horizon, called Land, the gateway is long forgotten among those who walked upright. Around it grows what has remained undisturbed for eons, aside from any unconcerning trespass to its nature.

About the Author

Keith Bingham has been traveling the dimensions of space and time for a little bit now, putting virtual pen to paper in the light of fantastical ways. At a clear attempt at rationality and reasoning, or perhaps an unbidden desire to be a world-class writer, Keith has lent his imagination to the idea of living forever and what that might mean for the people involved. Keith lives in beautiful Tennessee, after relocating from the cold and snowy state of New York and he says he likes it. Whether this means he likes leaving New York or likes living in Tennessee, it remains to be seen. Currently working on his second book, Keith enjoys the time he has with his family and two small dogs.

Visit the Author's Website
http://www.bamkaboom.co

www.ingramcontent.com/pod-product-compliance
Lightning Source LLC
Chambersburg PA
CBHW070535100726
47907CB00004B/1129